Edward A. Freeman

Sketches of Travel in Normandy and Maine

Edward A. Freeman

Sketches of Travel in Normandy and Maine

1st Edition | ISBN: 978-3-75237-265-6

Place of Publication: Frankfurt am Main, Germany

Year of Publication: 2020

Outlook Verlag GmbH, Germany.

SKETCHES OF TRAVEL

IN

NORMANDY AND MAINE

BY

EDWARD A. FREEMAN

PREFACE

"BEYOND doubt the finished historian must be a traveller: he must see with his own eyes the true look of a wide land; he must see, too, with his eyes the very spots where great events happened; he must mark the lie of a city, and take in, as far as a non-technical eye can, all that is special about a battle-field."

So wrote Mr. Freeman in his *Methods of Historical Study*,[1] and he possessed to the full the instincts of the traveller as well as of the historian. His studies and sketches of travels, already published, have shown him a wanderer in many lands and a keen observer of many peoples and their cities. He travelled always as a student of history and of architecture, and probably no man has ever so happily combined the knowledge of both. Though his thoughts were always set upon principles and upon the study of great subjects, he delighted in the details of local history and local building. "I cannot conceive," he wrote, "how either the study of the general sequence of architectural styles or the study of the history of particular buildings can be unworthy of the attention of any man. Besides their deep interest in themselves, such studies are really no small part of history. The way in which any people built, the form taken by their houses, their temples, their fortresses, their public buildings, is a part of their national life fully on a level with their language and their political institutions. And the buildings speak to us of the times to which they belong in a more living and, as it were, personal way than monuments or documents of almost any other kind."[2]

And no less clearly and decisively did he write of the value of local history: "There is no district, no town, no parish, whose history is not worth working out in detail, if only it be borne in mind that the local work is a contribution to a greater work."[3]

Thus the keenness of his interest in the architecture and the history that could be studied and learnt in every little town made him to the last the most untiring and enthusiastic of historical pilgrims. It is impossible to read his letters, so fresh and natural yet so full of a rare knowledge and insight, without seeing how thoroughly he had succeeded in achieving in himself that union of the traveller and the historian which adds so immeasurably to the powers of each. And that is what makes his letters from foreign lands so delightful to read, and his sketches (published and republished from time to time during the last thirty years) so illuminative. No one, I think, who has seen the places he writes of in his *Historical and Architectural Sketches* or in his *Sketches from French Travel*, with the books in his hand, will deny that

2

they have added tenfold to his pleasure. Mr. Freeman tells you what to see and how to see it,—just what you want to know and what you ought to know. It would be an impertinence in me to point out the breadth or the accuracy of his knowledge as it appears in these sketches, which can be read again and again with new pleasure. But I think it may be said without exaggeration that in all the great work that Mr. Freeman did he did nothing better than this. He never "writes down" to his readers: he expects to find in them something of his own interest in the buildings and their makers; and he supplies the knowledge which only the traveller who is also a historian has at hand.

The volume that is now published contains sketches written at different times from 1861 to 1891. It will be seen that they all bear more or less directly on the great central work of the historian's life, the history of the Norman Conquest. In his travels he went always to learn, and when he had learned he could not help teaching. The course of each of these journeys can be traced in his own letters as published in the *Life*. In 1856 he made his first foreign excursion—to Aquitaine—and after 1860 a foreign tour was "almost an annual event."[4] In 1861 he paid his first visit to Normandy, with the best of all companions. In 1867 he went again, specially for the sake of the "Norman Conquest," with Mr. J.R. Green and Mr. Sidney Owen; and in the next year he was in Maine with Mr. Green. In 1875 he was again in Normandy, for a short time, on his way to Dalmatia. In 1876 he went to Maine also to "look up the places belonging to"[5] William Rufus, and again in 1879 with Mr. J.T. Fowler and Mr. James Parker. In 1891 he paid his last visit to the lands which he had come to know so well. He was then thinking of writing on Henry I., a work of which he lived to write but little. In this last Norman journey the articles, published in *The Guardian* after his death, were written. His method on each of these expeditions seems to have been the same. Before he started he read something of the special history of the places he was to visit. He always, if possible, procured a local historian's book. He wrote his articles while he was still away. "To many of these Norman places," says his daughter who has prepared this volume for the press, "he went several times, and he never wearied of seeing them again himself or of showing them to others.... In the last Norman journey of 1891 how one feels he was at home there, re-treading the ground so carefully worked out for the Norman Conquest and William Rufus—the same enthusiasm with which, often under difficulties of weather or of health, he 'stepped out' all he could of Sicily."

Not only did he walk, and read, and write, while he was abroad, he drew: and from the hundreds of characteristic sketches which he has left it had been easy to select many more than those which now illustrate this volume. Still, from those that have been reproduced, with the descriptive studies just as they were written, the reader is in a position to see the Norman and Cenomannian sites as they were seen by the great historian himself. More remains from his hand, sketches of Southern Gaul, of Sicily, Africa, and Spain, which I hope may be republished; but the present volume has a unity of its own.

I have said thus much because it was the request of those who loved him best that I should say something here by way of preface, though I have no claim, historical or personal, that my name should in any way be linked with his. But the last of his many acts of kindness to me was the gift of his *Sketches from French Travel*, which had been recently published in the Tauchnitz edition. And as one of those who have used his travel-sketches with continued delight, who welcomed him to Oxford in 1884, and whose privilege it was to attend many of the lectures which he delivered as Professor, I speak, if without any claim, yet very gratefully and sincerely. And since his lectures illustrate so well the work which made his sketches so admirable, I may be suffered to say a word from my memory of them and of himself.

In his lectures on the text of mediæval historians he did a service to young students of history which was, in its way, unique. He showed them a great historian at work. In his comparison of authorities, in his references to and fro, in his appeal to every source of illustration, from fable to architecture, from poetry to charters, he made us familiar not only with his results, but with his methods of working. It was a priceless experience. Year after year he continued these lectures, informal, chatty, but always vigorous and direct, eager to give help, and keen to receive assistance even from the humblest of his hearers, choosing his subjects sometimes in connection with the historical work on which he happened to be engaged, sometimes in more definite relation to the subjects of the Modern History school. In this way he went through Gregory of Tours, Paul the Deacon—I speak only of those courses at which I was myself able to be present—and, in the last year of his life, the historians of the Saxon Emperors, 936–1002—Widukind, Thietmar, Richer, Liudprand, and the rest. In these and many other books, such as the Sicilian historians and the authorities for the Norman Conquest, he made the men and the times live again, and he seemed to live in them. Whatever the praise which students outside give to his published lectures, we who have listened to him and worked with him shall look back with fondness and gratitude most of all to those hours in his college rooms in Trinity, in the long, high dining-room in S. Giles's—the Judges' lodgings—and in the quaint low chamber in Holywell-street, where he fled for refuge when the Judges came to hold assize.

Much has been heard about Mr. Freeman's want of sympathy with modern Oxford, much that is mistaken and untrue. It is true that he loved most the Oxford of his young days, the Oxford of the Movement by which he was so profoundly influenced, the Oxford of the friends and fellow-scholars of his youth. But with no one were young students more thoroughly at home, from no one did they receive more keen sympathy, more generous recognition, or more friendly help. He did not like a mere smattering of literary chatter; he did not like to be called a pedant; but he knew, if any man did, what literature was and what was knowledge. He was eager to welcome good work in every field, however far it might be from his own.

It is true that Mr. Freeman was distinctly a conservative in academic matters, but it is quite a mistake to think that he was out of sympathy with modern Oxford. No man was more keenly alive to the good work of the younger generation. Certainly no man was more popular among the younger dons. A few, in Oxford and outside, snarled at him, as they snarl still, but they were very few who did not recognise the greatness of his character as well as of his powers. It is not too much to say of those who had been brought into at all near relations with him that they learnt not only to respect but to love him. He was—all came to recognise it—not only a distinguished historian, but, in the fullest sense of the words, a good man. He leaves behind him a memory of unswerving devotion to the ideal of learning—which no man placed higher than he. His remembrance should be an inspiration to every man who studies history in Oxford.

The kindness which allows me to say these words here is like his own, which was felt by the humblest of his scholars.

W.H. HUTTON.

NORMANDY

1861

BEFORE foreign travelling had become either quite so easy or quite so fashionable as it is now, the part of France most commonly explored by English tourists was Normandy. Antiquarian inquirers, in particular, hardly went anywhere else, and we suspect that with many of them a tour in France, as Mr. Petit says, still means merely a tour in Normandy.[6] The mere holiday tourist, on the other hand, now more commonly goes somewhere else—either to the Pyrenees or to those parts of France which form the road to Switzerland and Italy. The capital of the province, of course, is familiar to everybody; two of the chief roads to Paris lie through it. But Rouen, noble city as it is, does not fairly represent Normandy. Its buildings are, with small exceptions, later than the French conquest, and, as having so long been a capital, and now being a great manufacturing town, its population has always been very mixed. There are few cities more delightful to examine than Rouen, but for the true Normandy you must go elsewhere. The true Normandy is to be found further West. Its capital, we suppose we must say, is Caen; but its really typical and central city is Bayeux. The difference is more than nine hundred years old. In the second generation after the province became Normandy at all, Rouen had again become a French city. William Longsword, Rollo's son, sent his son to Bayeux to learn Danish. There the old Northern tongue, and, we fancy, the old Northern religion too, still flourished, while at Rouen nobody spoke anything but French.

A tour in Normandy has an interest of its own, but the nature of that interest is of a kind which does not make Normandy a desirable choice for a first visit to France. We will suppose that a traveller, as a traveller should, has learned the art of travel in his own land. Let him go next to some country which will be utterly strange to him—as we are talking of France, say Aquitaine or Provence. He will there find everything different from what he is used to— buildings, food, habits, dress, as unlike England as may be. If he tries to talk to the natives he will perhaps make them understand his *Langue d'oil*; but he will find that his Parisian grammar and dictionary will go but a very little way towards making him understand their *Lingua d'oc*. Now, Normandy and England, of course, have many points of difference, and doubtless a man who goes at once into Normandy from England will be mainly struck by the points of difference. But let a man go through Southern Gaul first, and visit Normandy afterwards, and he will be struck, not with the points of difference, but with the points of likeness. Buildings, men, beasts, everything will at once remind him of his own country. We hold that this is a very sufficient reason for visiting the more distant province first. Otherwise the very important phenomenon of the strong likeness between Normandy and England will not be taken in as it ought to be.

Go from France proper into Normandy and you at once feel that everything is palpably better. Men, women, horses, cows, all are on a grander and better scale. If we say that the food, too, is better, we speak it with fear and trembling, as food is, above all things, a matter of taste. From the point of view of a fashionable cook, no doubt the Norman diet is the worse, for whence should the fashionable cook come except from the land with which Normandy has to be compared? But certain it is that a man with an old-fashioned Teutonic stomach—a man who would have liked to dine off roast meat with Charles the Great or to breakfast off beef-steaks with Queen Elizabeth—will find Norman diet, if not exactly answering to his ideal, yet coming far nearer to it than the politer repasts of Paris. Rouen, of course, has been corrupted for nine centuries, but at Evreux, and in Thor's own city of Bayeux, John Bull may find good meat and good vegetables, and plenty of them to boot. Then look at those strong, well-fed horses—what a contrast to the poor, half-starved, flogged, over-worked beasts which usurp the name further south! Look at those goodly cows, fed in good pastures, and yielding milk thrice a day; they claim no sort of sisterhood with the poverty-stricken animals which, south of the Loire, have to do the horse's work as well as their own. Look at the land itself. An Englishman feels quite at home as he looks upon green fields, and, in the Bessin district, sees those fields actually divided by hedges. If the visitor chance not only to be an Englishman but a West-Saxon, he will feel yet more at home at seeing a land where the apple-tree takes the place of the vine, and where his host asks special payment for wine, but supplies "zider" for nothing. But above all things, look at the men. Those broad shoulders and open countenances seem to have got on the wrong side of the Channel. You are almost surprised at hearing anything but your own tongue come out of their mouths. It seems strange to hear such lips talking French; but it is something to think that it is at least not the French of Louis the Great or of Louis Napoleon, but the tongue of the men who first dictated the Great Charter, and who wrung its final confirmation from the greatest of England's later kings.

The truth is, that between the Englishman and the Norman—at least, the Norman of the Bessin—there can be, in point of blood, very little difference. One sees that there must be something in ethnological theories, after all. The good seed planted by the old Saxon and Danish colonists, and watered in aftertimes by Henry the Fifth and John, Duke of Bedford, is still there.[7] It has not been altogether choked by the tares of Paris. The word "Saxon" is so vague that we cannot pretend to say exactly who the Saxons of Bayeux were; but Saxons of some sort were there, even before another Teutonic wave came in with Rolf Ganger and his Northmen. Bayeux, as we have said, was the Scandinavian stronghold. Men spoke Danish there when not a word of Danish was understood at Rouen. Men there still ate their horse-steaks, and prayed to Thor and Odin, while all Rouen bowed piously at the altar of Notre-Dame. The ethnical elements of a Norman of the Bessin and an Englishman of Norfolk or Lincolnshire must be as nearly as possible the same. The only difference is, that one has quite forgotten his Teutonic speech, and the other only partially. Not that all Teutonic traces have gone even from the less Norman parts of Normandy. How many of the English travellers who land at Dieppe stop to think that the name of that port, disguised as it is by a French spelling, is nothing in the world but "The Deeps?" If any one, now that there is a railway, prefers to go along the lovely valley of the Seine, he will come to the little town of Caudebec. Here, again, the French spelling makes the word meaningless; but only write it "Cauld beck," and it at once tells its story to a Lowland Scot, and ought to do so to every "Anglo-Saxon" of any kind. As for the local dialect, it is French. It is not, like that of Aquitaine and Provence, a language as distinct as Spanish or Italian. It is French, with merely a dialectical difference from "French of Paris." But the Normans, in this resembling the Gascons, have no special objection to a final consonant, and most vulgarly and perversely still sound divers *s's* and *t's* which the politer tongue of the capital dooms to an existence on paper only.

It is certainly curious that Normandy—which, save during the comparatively short occupation in the fifteenth century, has always been politically separate from England, since England became English once more—should be so much more like England than Aquitaine, which was an English dependency two hundred and fifty years after Normandy and England were separated. The cause is clearly that between Englishmen and Normans there is a real natural kindred which political separation has not effaced, while between English and Gascons there was no sort of kindred, but a mere political connexion which chanced to be convenient for both sides. The Gascons, to this day, have not wholly forgotten the advantages of English connexion, but neither then nor now is any likeness to England the result. So, in our own time, we may hold Malta for ever, but we shall never make Maltese so like Englishmen as our Danish kinsmen still are without any political connexion more recent than the days of Earl Waltheof.

For the antiquary, nothing can be more fascinating than a Norman tour. Less curious, less instructive, because much more like English buildings, than those of Aquitaine, the architectural remains of the province are incomparably finer in themselves. Caen is a town well nigh without a rival. It shares with Oxford the peculiarity of having no one predominant object. At Amiens, at Peterborough—we may add at Cambridge—one single gigantic building lords it over everything. Caen and Oxford throw up a forest of towers and spires, without any one building being conspicuously predominant. It is a town which never was a Bishop's see, but which contains four or five churches each fit to have been a cathedral. There is the stern and massive pile which owes its being to the Conqueror of England, and where a life which never knew defeat was followed by a posthumous history which is only a long series of misfortunes. There is the smaller but richer minster, part of which at least is the genuine work of the Conqueror's Queen.[8] Around the town are a group of smaller churches such as not even Somerset or Northamptonshire can surpass. Then there is Bayeux, with its cathedral, its tapestry, its exquisite seminary chapel; Cerisy, with its mutilated but almost unaltered Norman abbey; Bernay, with a minster so shattered and desecrated that the traveller might pass it by without notice, but withal retaining the massive piers and arches of the first half of the eleventh century. There is Evreux, with its Norman naves, its tall slender Gothic choir, its strange Italian western tower, and almost more fantastic central spire. All these are noble churches, sharing with those of our own land a certain sobriety and architectural good sense which is often wanting in the churches of France proper. In Normandy as in England, you do not see piles, like Beauvais, begun on too vast a scale for man's labour ever to finish; you do not see piles like Amiens, where all external proportion is sacrificed to grandeur of internal effect.[9] A Norman minster, like an English one, is satisfied with a comparatively moderate height, but with its three towers and full cruciform shape, it seems a perfection of outline to which no purely French building ever attains.

FALAISE

1867

THE beginnings of the Norman Conquest, in its more personal and picturesque point of view, are to be found in the Castle of Falaise. There, as Sir Francis Palgrave sums up the story, "Arletta's pretty feet twinkling in the brook made her the mother of William the Bastard." And certainly, if great events depend upon great men, and if great men are in any way influenced by the places of their birth, there is no place which seems more distinctly designed by nature to be the cradle of great events. The spot is one which history would have dealt with unfairly if it had not contrived to find its way into her most striking pages. And certainly in this respect Falaise has nothing to complain of. Except one or two of the great cities of the province, no place is brought more constantly under our notice during five centuries of Norman history. And Norman history, we must not forget, includes in this case some of the most memorable scenes in the history of England, France, and Scotland. The siege by Henry the Fourth was in a manner local; it was part of a warfare within the kingdom of France. But that warfare was one in which all the Powers of Europe felt themselves to be closely interested; it was a warfare in which one at least of them directly partook; it was one in which the two great religions of Western Europe felt that their own fates were to be in a manner decided. In the earlier warfare of the fifteenth century Falaise plays a prominent part. Town and castle were taken and retaken, and the ancient fortress itself received a lasting and remarkable addition from the hand of one of the greatest of English captains. The tall round tower of Talbot, a model of the military masonry of its time, goes far to share the attention of the visitor with the massive keep of the ancient Dukes. Thence we leap back to the earliest great historical event which we can connect, with any certainty, with any part of the existing building. It was here, in a land beyond the borders of the Isle of Britain, but in a comparatively neighbouring portion of the wide dominions of the House of Anjou, that the fullest homage was paid which ever was paid by a King of Scots to a King of England. Here William the Lion, the captive of Alnwick, became most effectually the "man" of Henry Fitz-Empress, and burdened his kingdom with new and onerous engagements from which his next overlord found it convenient to relieve him. Earlier in the twelfth century, and in the eleventh, Falaise plays its part in the troubled politics of the Norman Duchy, in the wars of Henry the First and in the wars of his father. Still going back through a political and military history spread over so many ages, the culminating interest of Falaise continues to centre round its first historic mention. Henry of Navarre, our own Talbot, William the Lion, Robert of Bellême, all fail to kindle the same emotions as are aroused by the spot which was the favourite dwelling-place of the pilgrim of Jerusalem, the birthplace of the Conqueror of England.

Falaise Castle

Local tradition of course affirms the existing building to be the scene of William's birth. The window is shown from which Duke Robert first beheld the tanner's daughter, and the room in which William first saw what, if it really be the spot, must certainly have been light of an artificial kind. A pompous inscription in the modern French style calls on us to reverence the spot where the "legislator of ancient England" "fut engendré et naquit." The odd notion of William being the legislator of England calls forth a passing smile, and another somewhat longer train of thought is suggested. William, early in his reign, tried to learn English. He proved no very apt scholar, and he presently gave up his studies; but we may fairly believe that he learned enough to understand the simple formulæ of his own English charters. This leads one to ask the question: Would he not have been as likely to understand his own praises in the tongue of the conquered English as in what is supposed to represent his own native speech? Have we, after all, departed any further from the tongue of the oldest Charter of London than the Imperial dialect of abstractions and antitheses has departed from the simple and vigorous speech of the Roman de Rou? And, if he could spell it out in either tongue, he would find it somewhat faint praise to be told that, judged by the standard of the nineteenth century, he was a mere barbarian, but that M.F. Galeron would condescend so far as to suggest to his contemporaries to judge the local hero by a less rigid rule. If this is all the credit that the great William can get from his own people in his own birthplace, we can only say that, while demurring to his title of legislator of England, we would give him much better measure than this, even if we were writing on the site of the choir of Waltham.

Antiquaries have, till lately, generally acquiesced in the local belief that the existing building is the actual castle of Robert the Devil. The belief in no way commits us to the details of the local legend. Robert must have had an astonishingly keen sight if he could, from any window of the existing keep, judge of the whiteness of a pair of feet and ankles at the bottom of the rock. Nor does it at all follow that, if the present keep was standing at the time of William's birth, William was therefore born in it. The Duke's mistress would be just as likely to be lodged in some of the other buildings within the circuit of the castle as in the great square tower of defence. And, if we accept the belief, which is now becoming more prevalent, that the present keep is of the twelfth century and not of the eleventh, we are not thereby at all committed to the dogma that, because Robert the Devil lived before 1066, he could not possibly have had a castle of stone. In the wars of the eleventh and twelfth centuries many castles in Normandy were destroyed, not a few of them by William himself after the great revolt which was put down at <u>Val-ès-dunes</u>. The Norman castle, evidently of the type used after the Conquest, was introduced into England before the Conquest by the foreign favourites of Edward the Confessor. They could have built only in imitation of what they had been used to build in Normandy, and unless the new fashion, with its new name, had been a distinct advance on anything in the way of fortification already known in England, it would not have caused so much amazement as it did. Englishmen were perfectly familiar with stone walls to a town, but the Norman keep was something new, something for which there was no English name, and which therefore retained its French name of "castel." On the whole, the evidence is in favour of the belief that the present castle of Falaise is of the twelfth century. But there is no reason to deny, and there is every reason to believe, that Robert the Devil may have inhabited a castle of essentially the same type in the eleventh century.

Adjoining the keep is the tall round tower of the great Talbot. The two towers suggest exactly opposite remembrances. One sets before us the Norman dominant in England, the other sets before us the Englishman dominant in Normandy. Or the case may be put in another shape. Talbot, like so many of his comrades, was probably of Norman descent. Such returned to the land of their fathers in the character of Englishmen. And yet after all, when the descendants of Rolf's Danes and of the older Saxons of <u>Bayeux</u> assumed the character of Englishmen, they were but casting away the French husk and standing forth once more in the genuine character of their earlier forefathers. Such changes were doubtless quite unconscious; long before the fifteenth century the Norman in England had become thoroughly English, and the Norman in Normandy had become thoroughly French. French indeed in speech and manners he had been for ages, but by the time of Henry the Fifth he had become French in national feeling also. The tower of Talbot was no doubt felt by the people of Falaise to be a badge of bondage. It stands nobly and proudly, overtopping the older keep; its genuine masonry as good as on the day it was built, while the stuff with which its upper part was mended twenty years back has already crumbled away. Within, a few details of purely English character tell their tale in most intelligible language.

St Gervais, Falaise
S.W.

St. Gervase, Falaise, S.W.

The position of the castle is striking beyond measure. It is all the more so because it comes on the traveller who reaches the place in the way in which travellers are now most likely to reach it as a thorough surprise. In the approach by the railway the castle hardly shows at all. We pass through the streets of the town; the eye is caught by the splendid church of St. Gervase, but of the castle we get only the faintest glimpse, nothing at all to suggest the

14

full glory of its position. We pass on by the fine but very inferior church of the Holy Trinity; we contemplate the statue of the local hero; we pass through the castle gate; we pass by a beautiful desecrated chapel of the twelfth century; we feel by the rise of the ground and by the sight of the walks below that we are ascending, but it is not till we are close to the keep itself, till we have reached the very edge of the precipice, that we fully realise there is a precipice at all. At last we are on the brow; we see plainly enough the *falaises*, the *felsen*—the honest Teutonic word still surviving, and giving its name to the town itself, and to its distinguishing feature. The castle stands on the very edge of the steep and rugged rock; opposite to it frowns another mass of rocks, not sharp and peaked, but chaotic, like a mass of huge boulders rolled close together. From this point the English cannon played successfully on the ancient keep, which, under the older conditions of warfare, must have been well nigh impregnable. It is from this opposing height that the castle is now best surveyed by the peaceful antiquary. Between the two points tumbles along the same little beck in which the pretty feet are said to have twinkled, and not far off the trade of the damsel's father is still plied, perhaps on the very spot where that unsavoury craft, of old the craft of the demagogue, was so strangely to connect itself with the mightiest of Norman warriors and princes.

What, it may be asked, is the condition of this most interesting monument of an age which has utterly passed away? If there is any building in the world which belongs wholly to the past, towards which the duty of the present is simply to preserve, to guard every stone, to prop if need be, but to disturb nothing, to stay from falling as long as human power can stay it, but to abstain from supplanting one jot or one tittle of the ancient work by the most perfect of modern copies—it is surely the donjon-keep of Falaise. But, like every other building in France, the birthplace of the Conqueror is hopelessly handed over to the demon of restoration. They who have turned all the ancient monuments of France upside down have come to Falaise also. They who were revelling ten years back in the destruction of Périgueux, they who are even now fresh from effacing all traces of antiquity from the noble minster of Matilda, they who have thrust their own handiworks even into the gloomy crypt of Odo, have at last stretched forth their hands to smite the cradle of the Conqueror himself. The Imperial architect, M. Ruprich Robert, has surveyed the building, he has drawn up a most clear and intelligent account of its character and history, and, on this showing, the work of destruction has begun. Controversy will soon be at an end; there will be no need to dispute whether any part be of the eleventh or of the twelfth century; both alike are making room for a spruce imitation of the nineteenth. We shall no longer see the dwelling-place either of Robert the Devil or of Henry Fitz-Empress; in its stead we shall trace the last masterpiece of the reign of Napoleon the Third. Sham Romanesque is grotesque everywhere, but it is more grotesque than all when we see newly-cut capitals stuck into the windows of a roofless castle, when the grey hue of age is wiped away from a building which has stood at least seven hundred years, and when the venerable fortress is made to look as spick and span as the last built range of shops at Paris. Among the endless pranks, at once grotesque and lamentable, played by the mania for restoration, surely the "restoration" of this venerable ruin is the most grotesque and lamentable of all. The municipality of Caen have lately made themselves a spectacle to mankind by pulling down, seemingly out of sheer wantonness, one half of one of the most curious churches of their city.[10] We commend them not; but we do not place even them on a level with the subtler destroyers of Falaise. The savages of Caen are satisfied with simple, open destruction; what they cannot understand or appreciate they make away with. But there is no hypocrisy, no pretence about them; they simply destroy, they do not presume to replace. But the restorer not only takes away the work of the men of old, he impudently puts his own work in its stead. He takes away the truth and puts a lie in its place. Our readers know very well with what reservations this doctrine must be taken—reservations which in the case of churches or other buildings actually applied to appropriate modern uses, are very considerable. But in the case of a mere monument of antiquity, a building whose only value is that it has stood so many years, that it exhibits the style of such an age, that it has beheld such and such great events, there is no reservation to be made at all. In the castle of Falaise we may adopt, word for word, the most vehement of Mr. Ruskin's declamations on this head. The man who turns the ancient reality of the twelfth century into a sham of the nineteenth deserves no other fame than the fame which Eratostratus won at Ephesus, and which James Wyatt won in the chapter-house of Durham.

THE CATHEDRAL CHURCHES OF BAYEUX, COUTANCES, AND DOL

1867

One would rather like to see a map of France, or indeed of Europe, marking in different degrees of colour the abundance or scarcity of English visitors and residents. Of course the real traveller, whether he goes to study politics or history or language or architecture or anything else, is best pleased when he gets most completely out of the reach of his own countrymen. The first stage out of the beaten track of tourists is a moment of rapture. For it is the tourists who do the mischief; the residents are a comparatively harmless folk. A colony of English settled down in a town and its neighbourhood do very little to spoil the natives among whom they live. For the very reason that they are residents and not tourists, they do not in the same way corrupt innkeepers, or turn buildings and prospects into vulgar lions. It is hard to find peace at Rouen, as it is hard to find it at Aachen; but a few English notices in the windows at Dinan do not seriously disturb our meditations beneath the spreading apses of St. Sauveur and St. Malo or the plaster statue of Bertrand du Guesclin. For any grievances arising from the neighbourhood of our countrymen, we might as well be at Dortmund or Rostock. But, between residents, tourists, and real travellers, we may set it down that there is no place which Englishmen do not visit sometimes, as there certainly are many places in which Englishmen abound more than enough.

We have wandered into this not very profound or novel speculation through a sort of wish to know how far three fine French churches of which we wish to speak a few words are respectively known to Englishmen in general. These are the Norman cathedrals of Bayeux and Coutances, both of them still Bishops' sees, and the Breton Cathedral of Dol, which, in the modern ecclesiastical arrangements, has sunk into a parish church. Bayeux lies on a great track, and we suppose that all the world goes there to see the tapestry. Coutances has won a fame among professed architectural students almost higher than it deserves, but we fancy that the city lies rather out of the beat of the ordinary tourist. Dol is surely quite out of the world; we trust that, in joining it with the other two, we may share somewhat of the honours of discovery. We will not say that we trust that no one has gone thither from the Greater Britain since the days of the Armorican migration; but we do trust that a criticism on the cathedral church of Dol will be somewhat of a novelty to most people.

We select these three because they have features in common, and because they all belong to the same general type of church. As cathedrals, they are all of moderate size; Coutances and Dol, we may distinctly say, are of small size. They do not range with such miracles of height as France shows at Amiens and Beauvais, or with such miracles of length as England shows at Ely and St. Albans. They rank rather with our smaller episcopal churches, such as Lichfield, Wells, and Hereford. Indeed most of the great Norman churches come nearer to this type than to that of minsters of a vaster scale. And the reason is manifest. The great churches of Normandy, like those of England, are commonly finished with the central tower. Perhaps they do not always make it a feature of quite the same importance which it assumes in England, but it gives them a marked character, as distinguished from the great churches of the rest of France. Elsewhere, the central tower, not uncommon in churches of the second and third rank, is altogether unknown among cathedrals and other great minsters of days later than Romanesque. It is as much the rule for a French cathedral to have no central tower as it is for an English or Norman cathedral to have one. The result is that, just as in our English churches, the enormous height of Amiens and Beauvais cannot be reached. But, in its stead, the English and Norman churches attained a certain justness of proportion and variety of outline which the other type does not admit. No church in Normandy, except St. Ouen's, attains any remarkable height, and even St. Ouen's is far surpassed by many other French churches. But perhaps a vain desire to rival the vast height of their neighbours sometimes set the Norman builders to attempt something of comparative height by stinting their churches in the article of breadth. This peculiarity may be seen to an almost painful extent at Evreux.

Coutances Cathedral, Central Tower

Our three churches, then—Coutances and Dol certainly—rank with our smaller English cathedrals, allowing for a greater effect of height, partly positive, partly produced by narrowness. They are, in fact, English second-class churches with the height of English first-class churches. Bayeux, in every way the largest of the three, perhaps just trembles on the edge of the first-class. Coutances, the smallest, is distinctly defective in length; the magnificent, though seemingly unfinished, central tower, plainly wants a longer eastern limb to support it. Even at Bayeux the eastern limb is short according to English notions, though not so conspicuously so as Coutances. We suspect that Dol is really the most justly proportioned of the three, though in many points its outline is the one which would least commend itself to popular taste. The central tower is still lower than that at Lisieux; it is rather like that of St. Canice at Kilkenny, only just rising above the level of the roof.

But, as is always the case with this arrangement, the effect is solemn and impressive. The low heavy central tower is a common feature in Normandy, and one to which the eye soon gets accustomed. The west front of Dol is imperfect and irregular; the southern has been carried up and finished in a later style, while the northern one, whose rebuilding had been begun, was left unfinished altogether. The whole front is mutilated and poor, and the chief attractions of Dol must be looked for elsewhere. The west front of Coutances is as famous as the west front of Wells, and both, to our taste, equally undeservedly. Both are shams; in neither does a good, real, honest gable stand out between the two towers. The west front of Coutances also is a mass of meaningless breaks and projections, and the form of the towers is completely disguised by the huge excrescences in the shape of turrets. Far finer, to our taste, is the front of Bayeux. Though it is a composition of various dates, thrown together in a sort of casual way, and though the details of the two towers do not exactly agree, yet the different stages are worked together so as to produce a very striking effect. The later work seems not so much to be stuck upon the earlier as to grow out of it. One could hardly have thought that spires, among the most elegant of the elegant spires of the district, would have looked so thoroughly in place as they do when crowning towers, the lower parts at least of which are the work of the famous Odo. There is nothing of that inconsistency which is clearly marked between the upper and lower parts of the front of St. Stephen's at Caen. The general external effect of Bayeux can hardly be judged of till the completion of the new central lantern. This last is a bold experiment, seemingly a Gothic version of the cupola which it displaces. But as far as the original work goes, there can be no doubt of Bayeux holding much the first place among our three churches.

Interior of Coutances Cathedral

Looked at within, the precedence of Bayeux is less certain. The first glance at Coutances, within as without, is disappointing, mainly because the visitor has been led to expect a building on a grander scale. But the interior soon grows on the spectator, in a way in which the outside certainly does not. The first impression felt is one of being cramped for room. The difference between Coutances and Bayeux is plainly shown by the fact that at Bayeux room is found for a spacious choir east of the central tower, while at Coutances a smaller choir is driven to annex the space under the lantern. This is an arrangement which is often convenient in any case, but which, as a matter of effect, commonly suits a Romanesque church better than a Gothic one. But when we come more thoroughly to take in the internal beauties of Coutances, we begin to feel that Bayeux, with all its superior grandeur, has found a very formidable rival. Coutances is the more harmonious whole. The choir and the nave vary considerably, and the choir must be somewhat the later of the two. But the difference is hardly of a kind to interfere much with the general effect. The general appearance of the church is thoroughly consistent throughout, and the octagon lantern, with its arcades, galleries, and pendentives, all open to the church, forms a magnificent feature. It is evidently the feature of which Coutances was specially proud; it is repeated, at a becoming distance, in the other two churches of the city, as well as elsewhere in the diocese. The nave arcades of Coutances are exquisite, the triforium is well proportioned and well designed, except that perhaps the beautiful floriated devices in the head may be thought to have usurped the place of some more strictly architectural design. The clerestory is perhaps a little heavy. In the choir the clerestory and triforium are thrown into one stage of singular likeness, though in this style the lack of a distinct triforium is always to be regretted. The mouldings in both parts have, as is so usual in Normandy, an English look, which is quite unknown in France proper, and in the choir we find a larger use of the characteristic English round abacus. But, next to the lantern, the most striking thing in the interior of Coutances is certainly the sweep of the eastern aisles and chapels, where the interlacing aisles and pillars produce an effect of spaciousness which is not to be found in the main portions of the church.

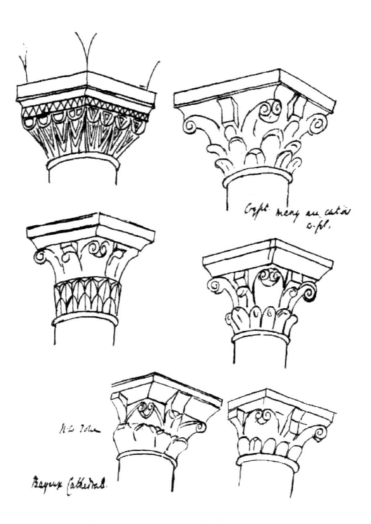

Capitals in Bayeux Cathedral

The interior of Bayeux, besides its greater spaciousness and grandeur of effect, is attractive on other grounds. It is far more interesting than Coutances to the historical inquirer. Many facts in the history of Normandy are plainly written in the architectural changes of this noble church. The most interesting portion indeed does not appear in the general view of the interior. The church of Odo, the church at whose dedication William was present, and which must have been rising at the time of the visit of Harold, now survives only in the crypt of the choir and in the lower portions of the towers.[1111] The rest was destroyed by fire, like so many other churches in Normandy, during the wars of Henry the First. Of the church which then replaced it, the arcades of the nave still remain. No study of Romanesque can be more instructive than a comparison of the work of these two dates. Odo's work is plain and simple, with many of the capitals of a form eminently characteristic of an early stage of the art of floriated enrichment—a form of its own which grew up alongside of others, and gradually budded into such splendid capitals of far later work as we see at Lisieux. Will it be believed that the remorseless demon of restoration has actually descended the steps of this venerable crypt, and that two of the capitals are now, not of the eleventh century, but brand-new productions of the nineteenth? Of course we are told that they are exact copies; but what then? We do not want copies, but the things themselves, and if they were a little ragged and jagged, what harm could it do down underground?

A striking contrast to the work of Odo, a contrast as striking as can easily be found between two things which are, after all, essentially of the same style, is to be seen in the splendid arcades of the nave, one of the richest examples to be found anywhere of the later and more ornamented Romanesque. The arches are of unusual and very irregular width; the irregularity must be owing to something in the remains or foundations of the earlier building. They are crowned, however, not by a triforium and clerestory of their own style, but a single clerestory of coupled lancets of enormous height, with the faintest approach to tracery in the head. The effect is striking, but certainly somewhat incongruous. The choir is one of the most beautiful productions of the thirteenth-century style of the country, always approaching nearer to English work than the architecture of any other part of the Continent. Another church at Bayeux, that which now forms the chapel of the seminary, is well known as being more English still. It might, as far as details go, stand unaltered as an English building.

And now for a few words as to the obscure Breton church which we have ventured to put into competition with such formidable Norman rivals.[12] Perhaps it derives some of its attractions from its being out of the way and comparatively unknown. It has that peculiar charm which attaches to a fine building found where one would hardly expect to find it—a feeling which reaches its highest point at St. David's. The first impression which it gives is that there is something Irish about it; there is certainly no church in Ireland which can be at all compared to it; still it is something like what one could fancy St. Canice growing into. One marked characteristic of Dol Cathedral comes from its material. It is built of the granite of the country, which necessarily gives it a somewhat stern and weather-beaten look, and hinders any great exuberance of architectural ornament. Not that we think this any loss; the simple buttresses and flying buttresses at Dol are really a relief after the elaborate and unintelligible forests of pinnacles which surround so many French churches, even of very moderate size. It is only in the huge porch attached to the south transept that an approach to anything of this kind is found. But very beautiful work of other sorts may be seen at Dol. The smaller porch is a gem of early work, and the range of windows in the north aisle presents some of the most delicate triumphs of geometrical tracery, too delicate in truth to last, as all are more or less broken. The flat east end gives the church an English look, and the flat east end with an apsidal chapel beyond it especially suggests Wells. Within, the church has a great effect of height and narrowness, greater certainly than Coutances. Like Coutances, the nave and choir are of somewhat different dates, the choir being more modern, but, unlike Coutances, still more unlike Bayeux, they range completely together in composition. The nave we might fairly call Early English. It is not quite so characteristic as some of the work at Bayeux, but it uses the round abacus freely, although not exclusively. But for a few square abaci which are used, and for the appearance of early tracery in the side windows, it might pass as a purely Lancet building. The choir is fully developed geometrical work, of excellent character, with a beautifully designed triforium and clerestory. Altogether we think Dol may make good its claim to a high place among churches of the second order. It is specially curious to see how a building which does not differ in any essential peculiarity of style from its fellows assumes a distinct character, and that by no means wholly to its loss, through the use of a somewhat rugged material.

OLD NORMAN BATTLE-GROUNDS

1867

In the strictly historical aspect, the English inquirer is perhaps naturally led to think most of those events in which his more recent countrymen were more immediately concerned—those events of the Hundred Years' War, on which so much light has lately been thrown by the researches of M. Puiseux.[13] But he should not forget that, besides being the scene of these events in the great struggle between England and France, Normandy, independent Normandy, has also a history of its own, in which both England and France had a deep interest. It is not only because Normandy is the cradle of so many families which after events made English, because so many Norman villages still bear names illustrious in the English peerage. It is because it is in the earlier history of Normandy, above all, in the reign of William himself, that we are to seek for one side of the causes which made a Norman conquest of England possible, just as it is in the earlier history of England, above all, in the reign of Eadward, that we are to seek for the other side of those causes.

No one among those causes was more important than the personal character of the great Duke of the Normans himself. And the qualities which made William able to achieve the Conquest of England were, if not formed, at least trained and developed, by the events of his reign in his own Duchy. Succeeding with a very doubtful title, at once bastard and minor, it is wonderful that he contrived to retain his ducal crown at all; it is not at all wonderful that his earlier years were years of constant struggle within and without his dominions. He had to contend against rivals for the Duchy, and against subjects to whom submission to any sovereign was irksome. He had to contend against a jealous feudal superior, who dreaded his power, who retained somewhat of national dislike to the Danish intruders, and who, shut up in his own Paris, could hardly fail to grudge to any vassal the possession of the valley and mouth of the Seine. William, in short, before he conquered England, had to conquer both Normandy and France. And such was his skill, such was his good luck, that he found out how to conquer Normandy by the help of France, and how to conquer France by the help of Normandy. The King of the French acted as his ally against his rebellious vassals, and those rebellious vassals changed into loyal subjects when it was needful to withstand the aggressions of the King of the French.

The principal stages in this warfare are marked by two battles, the sites of which are appropriately placed on the two opposite sides of the Seine. At Val-ès-dunes William of Normandy and Henry of France overcame the Norman rebels.[14] Afterwards, when Henry had changed his policy, the Normans smote the French with a great slaughter at Mortemer, neither of the contending princes being personally present. Val-ès-dunes, we must confess the fact, was in truth a victory of the Roman over the Teuton. It was by the aid of his French overlord that William chastised into his obedience the sturdy Saxons of the Bessin and the fierce Danes of the Côtentin. The men of the peninsula boasted, in a rhyme which is still not forgotten in the neighbourhood of the fight, how

> De Costentin partit la lance
> Qui abastit le roy de France.

For King Henry, successful in the general issue of the day, had his own personal mishaps in the course of the battle, and to have overthrown the King of the French was an exploit which supplied the vanquished with some little consolation.

The scene of this battle is fitly to be found in the true Normandy, but towards its eastern frontier. It must not be forgotten that the truest Normandy was not the oldest Normandy. The lands first granted to Rolf, perhaps for the very reason that they were the lands first granted to him, became French, while the later acquisitions of Rolf himself still remained Danish.

The boundary was seemingly marked by the Dive. Val-ès-dunes then, placed a little to the west of that river, comes within the true Normandy, though it is near to its outskirts. The Teutonic Norman was beaten on his own ground, but the Frenchman at least never made his way to the gates of Bayeux or Coutances. The site of the battle is less attractive to the eye than many other battle-fields, but the ground is excellently adapted for what the battle seems really to have been, a sharp encounter of cavalry, a few gallant charges ending in the headlong flight of the defeated side. This was the young Duke's first introduction to serious warfare; but he had tougher work than this to go through before his career was over. To the east of Caen stretches a somewhat dreary country, which forms a striking contrast to the rich meadows and orchards of the Bessin, while it in no way approaches to the wildness of the sterner portions of the Côtentin. A range of hills of some height bounds the prospect to the north, and it was from that direction that William brought his forces to the field. The field itself is a sort of low plateau, sloping to the east, and bordered by a series of villages placed in what, if the height of the rising ground were higher, might be called *combes* or valleys. The churches of Valmeray, where a ruined fragment of later date marks the spot where King Henry heard mass before the fight, Billy, Boneauville, Chicheboville, and Secqueville, all skirt the hill, if hill we can call it. The actual battle-field lies

27

between the two last-named villages. To the west a higher ridge, called by the name of St. Lawrence, marks the furthest point of the battle, the place where the defeated rebels made their last stand, and which was marked by a commemorative chapel, now destroyed. From that point the high ground again stretches westward as far as the village of Haute Allemagne, the great quarry of Caen stone. Over all the ground in this direction the rebels were scattered, multitudes of them being carried away, we are told, by the stream of the Orne.

The spot, as we have said, is not in itself particularly attractive, though there is something striking in the view both ways from the high ground of St. Lawrence. It is easy to say how thoroughly well the ground was chosen for what took place on it, a *mêlée*, of mounted knights, a tournament in earnest. And it is quite worth the while of any student of Norman history to walk over the ground, Wacc in hand, taking in the graphic description of the honest rhymer, as clear and accurate as usual in his topographical details. And it is pleasant to find how well the events of the day are still remembered by the peasantry of the neighbourhood. There is no fear, as there is said to be in the neighbourhood of Worcester, of an inquirer after the field of battle being taken to see the scene of a battle between some local Sayers and Heenan. The Norman of every rank, when let alone by Frenchmen, is a born antiquary, proud of the ancient history of his country, and taking an intelligent interest in it which in England is seldom to be found except amongst highly-educated men.

The other site, Mortemer, lies in a region far more attractive to the eye than Val-ès-dunes, but, as an historical spot, it is chiefly remarkable from the event of the battle having, so to speak, wiped out all traces of itself.[15] The spot where the French invaders received so heavy a blow lies appropriately in the more French part of Normandy, in the region on the right of the Seine, and it seems to have been almost wholly by the hands of the men of the surrounding districts that the blow was struck. The Mortemer of which we speak must not be mistaken for the Abbey of Mortemer, near Lyons-la-forêt, in that famous wood of which Sir Francis Palgrave has so much to tell. Both the one and the other Mortemer happily lie quite out of the beat of ordinary tourists. The Mortemer of the battle lies on the road between the small towns of Neufchâtel and Aumale. Neufchâtel-en-Bray, a Neufchâtel without lake or watches or republic, can nevertheless boast of surrounding hills which, if not equal to the Jura, are of considerable height for Northern Gaul, and its cheese is celebrated through a large portion of Normandy. Ascend and descend one hill, then ascend and descend another, and the journey is made from Neufchâtel to Aumale. Just out of the road, at the base of the two hills, the eye is caught by a ruined tower on the right hand. This is what remains of the castle of

Mortemer, a fragment of considerably later date than the battle. The church is modern and worthless; the few scattered houses, almost wholly of wood, which form the hamlet, present nothing remarkable. But it is in this very absence of anything remarkable that the historic interest of Mortemer consists. The Mortemer of the eleventh century was a town; the Mortemer of the nineteenth century is a very small and scattered village. Doubtless a town of that age might be, in point of population, not beyond a village now; still a town implies continuous houses, which is just what Mortemer now does not possess. The French occupied Mortemer because of the convenient quarters to be had in its hostels. It is now one of the last places in the world to which one would go for quarters of any kind. Mortemer was apparently an open town, not defended by walls or a castle, or the French could hardly have occupied it, as they did, without resistance. But it must have been a town, as towns then went, or so large a body could not have been so comfortably quartered in it as they evidently were. The key to the change is to be found in the event itself. The Normans of the surrounding country surprised the French on the morning after they had entered Mortemer, while they were still engaged in revelry and debauchery. They set fire to the town, and slew the Frenchmen as they attempted to escape. To all appearance, the town was never rebuilt, and its change into the mean collection of houses which now bears its name is a strange but abiding trophy of a great triumph of Norman craft—in this case we can hardly say of Norman valour—eight centuries back.

Such are two of the historic spots which are to be found in abundance on the historic soil of Normandy. They are only two out of many; every town, almost every village, has its tale to tell. From Eu to Pontorson there is hardly a spot which does not make some contribution to the history of those stirring times when Normandy had a life of its own, and when the Norman name was famous from Scotland to Sicily. After six hundred years of incorporation with the French monarchy, Normandy is still Norman; "le Duc Guillaume" is still a familiar name, not only to professed scholars or antiquaries, but to the people themselves. Without any political bearing—for the political absorption of Normandy by France was remarkably speedy—the feelings and memories of the days of independence have lingered on in a way which is the more remarkable as there is no palpable distinction of language, such as distinguishes Bretons, Basques, or even the speakers of the Tongue of Oc. But in everything but actual speech the old impress remains, and the result is that in Normandy, above all in Lower Normandy, the English historical traveller finds himself more thoroughly at home than in any other part of the Continent except in the lands where the speech once common to England, to Bayeux, and to Northern Germany is still preserved.

FÉCAMP

1868

It has sometimes struck us that the mediæval founders of towns and castles and monasteries were not so wholly uninfluenced by considerations of mere picturesque beauty as we are apt to fancy. We are apt to think that they had nothing in their minds but mere convenience, according to their several standards of convenience, convenience for traffic, convenience for military defence or attack, convenience for the chase, the convenience of solitude in one class of ecclesiastical foundations, the convenience of the near neighbourhood of large centres of men in another class. This may be so; but, if so, these considerations of various kinds constantly led them, by some sort of happy accident, to the choice of very attractive sites. And we venture to think that it was not merely accident, because we often come upon descriptions of sites in mediæval writers which seem to show that the men of those times were capable of appreciating the picturesque position of this or that castle or abbey, as well as its direct suitableness for military or monastic purposes. Giraldus, for instance, evidently admired the site of Llanthony, and, if he expressed himself about it in rather exaggerated language, that is no more than what naturally happens when any man, especially when Giraldus, expresses himself in Latin, especially in mediæval Latin. In the like sort, we have come across one or two descriptions of the Abbey of Fécamp which clearly show that the writers were struck, as any man of taste would be, with the position in which that great and famous monastery had arisen. And, to leap to scenes which far surpass either Fécamp or Llanthony, the well-known story of Saint Bernard's absorption on the shores of the Lake of Geneva really tells the other way. We are told that the saint was so given up to pious contemplation that he travelled for a whole day through that glorious region without noticing lake, mountains, or anything else. Now we need hardly stop to show that the fact that Bernard's absorption was thought worthy of record proves that, if he did not notice any of these things, there was some one in his company who did. We suspect that in this, as in a great many things, we have more in common with our forefathers several centuries back than we have with those who are nearer to us by many generations.

Abbey of Fécamp, N.E.

Modern taste might possibly make one objection to the site of Fécamp. Though near the sea, it is not within sight of the sea. The modern watering-place of Fécamp is springing up at a considerable distance from the ancient abbey. But the love of watering-places and sea-bathing is one which is altogether modern, and, in the days in which our old towns, castles, and monasteries grew up, a site immediately on the sea would have been looked on as unsafe. And in truth there are not many places, and certainly Fécamp is not one of them, where all the various buildings of a great monastery could have been planned so as to command the modern attraction of a sea-view. Moreover it is a point not to be forgotten that people who go to Fécamp or elsewhere for sea-views and sea-bathing go there during certain months only, while the monks had to live there all the year round. The monks of Saint Michael's Mount were indeed privileged with, or condemned to, an everlasting sea-view; but the title of their house was that of Saint Michael "*in periculo maris.*" To be exposed to the perils of the sea was no part of the intention of the founders of Fécamp, either of abbey, town or palace.[16] They chose them a site which gave them the practical advantages of the sea without the dangers of its immediate neighbourhood. Fécamp then lies a little way inland. Two parallel ranges of hills run down to the sea, with a valley and a small stream between them, at the mouth of which the modern port has been made. On the slope of the hills on the left side lies the huge mass of the minster rising over the long straggling town which stretches away to the water. But though the great church thus lies secluded from the sea, the spiritual welfare of sea-faring men was not forgotten. The point where the opposite range of hills directly overhangs the sea is crowned by one of those churches specially devoted to sailors and their pilgrimages which are so often met with in such positions. The chapel of Our Lady of Safety, now restored after a season of ruin and desecration, forms a striking and picturesque object in the general landscape. And from the chapel itself and from the hill-side paths which lead up to it, we get the noblest views of the great abbey, in all the stern simplicity of its age, stretching the huge length of its nave, one of the very few, even in Normandy, which rival the effect of Winchester and Saint Albans. A single central tower, of quite sufficient height, of no elaborate decoration, crowned by no rich spire or octagon, but with a simple covering of lead, forms the thoroughly appropriate centre of the whole building. We feel that this tower is exactly what is wanted; we almost doubt whether the church gained or lost by the loss of the western towers, which would have taken off from the effect of boundless length which is the characteristic of the building. At any rate we think how far more effective is the English and Norman arrangement, which at all events provides a great church with the noblest of central crowns, than the fashion of France, which concentrates all its force on the western front, and leaves the at least equally important point of crossing to shift for itself.

The church itself is one of the noblest even in Normandy, and it is in remarkably good preservation. And the two points in which the fabric has suffered severe damage are not owing either to Huguenots or to Jacobins, but to its own guardians under two different states of things. The bad taste of the monks themselves in their later days is chargeable with the ugly Italian west front, which has displaced the elder front with towers of which the stumps may still be seen. An Italian front, though it must be incongruous when attached to a mediæval building, need not be in itself either ugly or mean, but this front of Fécamp is conspicuously both. The other loss is that of the *jubé* or roodloft, which, from the fragments left, seems to have been a magnificent piece of later Gothic work, perhaps almost rivalling the famous one at Alby. The destruction of roodlofts has been so general in France that one is not particularly struck by each several case of destruction. But there is something singular about this Fécamp case, as the *jubé* was pulled down at the restoration of religion, through the influence of the then curé, in opposition to the wishes of his more conservative or more ritualistic parishioners. With these two exceptions Fécamp has lost but little, as far as regards the church itself. The conventual buildings, like most French conventual buildings, have been rebuilt in an incongruous style, and now serve for the various public purposes of the local administration. In a near view of the north side, they form an ugly excrescence against the church, but they are lost in the more distant and general view.

The church itself mainly belongs to the first years of the thirteenth century, with smaller portions both of earlier and of later date. On entering the church, we find that the long western limb is not all strictly nave, the choir, by an arrangement more common in England than in France, stretching itself west of the central tower. The whole of this western limb is built in the simplest and severest form of that earliest French Gothic, which to an English eye seems to be simply an advanced form of the transition from Romanesque. Even at Amiens, amid all the splendours of its fully-developed geometrical windows, the pillars and arches, in their square abaci and even in the sections of their mouldings, have what an Englishman calls a Romanesque feeling still hanging about them. At Fécamp this is far stronger. The large triforium, the untraceried windows, the squareness of everything except a few English round abaci in some bays of the triforium, the external heaviness and simplicity, all make the early Gothic of Fécamp little more than pointed Romanesque. We do not say this in disparagement. This stage was a necessary stage for architecture to pass through, and the Transitional period is always one of the most interesting in architectural history. And when work of that date is carried out with such excellence both of composition and detail as it is at Fécamp, it is much more than historically interesting, it is thoroughly satisfactory in artistic effect. We say nothing against the style, except that, as being essentially imperfect and not realising the ideal of either of the two styles between which it comes historically, we cannot look on it as a proper model for modern imitation. Several diversities of detail may on minute examination be seen in the different bays of the nave of Fécamp, just as in the contemporary nave of Wells. Just as at Wells, the western part—in this case the five western bays—is slightly later than the rest. And, as at Wells, the distinction between the older and newer work is easily to be remarked by those who look for it, though it is a distinction which makes no difference in the general effect and which might pass unnoticed by any but a very minute observer. In truth it is, in both cases, a difference not of style but of taste. The eastern limb of Fécamp—strictly the presbytery and not the choir—is more remarkable in some ways than the nave. It is here that we find the only remains of an earlier church, and these are of no very remarkable antiquity. M. Bouet, in a short account of Fécamp, addressed to the Norman Antiquarian Society, records his disappointment at finding at Fécamp no traces of the days of the early Dukes, or even of days earlier still, such as he found at Jumièges.

This oldest part of Fécamp is part of a church begun so late as 1085. One bay of its presbytery and two adjoining chapels have been spared. The style is a little singular. There is something not quite Norman about the very square arches of a single order, and the capitals are not the usual Norman capitals of the second half of the eleventh century. Except this bay, the presbytery has been rebuilt in essentially the same style as the nave, though naturally a little earlier. But on the south side a singular change took place in the fourteenth century. As at Waltham, the builders of that day cut away the triforium and threw the two lower stages into one. But what was done at Waltham in the most awkward and bungling way in which anything ever was done anywhere, was at Fécamp at least done very cleverly. Without meddling with the vaulting or the vaulting-shafts, the pier-arches and triforium range of the thirteenth century have been changed into arches of the fourteenth, resting on tall slender pillars, almost recalling the choir of Le Mans. Whether this change was an improvement or not is a question of taste, but there can be no question as to the wonderful skill, æsthetical and mechanical, with which the change was made, and it is the more striking from the contrast with the wretched "botch" at Waltham.

The church is finished to the east by a fine Flamboyant Lady Chapel. The contrast between it and the earlier work suggests the effect of Henry the Seventh's Chapel at Westminster, though the contrast is not quite so strong. Altogether there can be no doubt of the claim of the church to a place in the very first rank of the great minsters of a province specially rich in such works.

We have dwelt so long on the position and the architecture of Fécamp that we have no space left to add anything on its history. But the local history of Fécamp naturally connects itself with several other more general points at which we shall perhaps have some future opportunity of glancing.

FOOTSTEPS OF THE CONQUEROR

1868

MANY of the great events of Norman history, many of the chief events in the life of the Great William, happened conveniently in or near to the great cities of the Duchy. But many others also happened in somewhat out of the way places, which no one is likely to get to unless he goes there on purpose. The Conqueror received his death-wound at Mantes, he died in a suburb of Rouen, he was buried at Caen. All these are places easy to get at. Perhaps we should except Mantes, which in a certain sense is not easy to get at. All the world goes by Mantes, but few people stop there. The reason is manifest. The traveller who goes by Mantes commonly has in his pocket a ticket for Paris, which enables him to spend a day at Rouen, but not to spend a day at Mantes. People very anxious to stop at Mantes, and to muse, so to speak, among its embers, have had great searchings of heart how to get there, and have not accomplished their object till after some years of reflection. And the interest of Mantes, after all, is mainly negative. The town stands well; its river, its bridges, its islands, suggest the days when Scandinavian pirates sailed up the Seine and encamped with special delight on such *eys* or *holms* as that between Mantes and Limay. A specially prolonged fit of musing may perhaps lead one to regret the prowess of Count Odo, and to wish that Paris also had received that wholesome Northern infusion which still works so healthily between the Epte and the Coesnon. But Mantes, as regards William, is something like Mortemer as regards William's rival King Henry. Mantes can show no traces of William or his age, for the simple reason that William took good care that no such traces should be left. By perhaps the worst deed of his life, a deed which awakened special indignation at the time, he gave Mantes to destruction to avenge a silly jest of its sovereign. At Mantes he held his churching and lighted his candles, and their blaze burned up houses, churches, whatever was there. Therefore, because William himself was there in only too great force, it is that Mantes has no work of man to show on which William can ever have looked. The church, whose graceful towers every one has seen from the railway, is a grand fabric a hundred years or more later than William's time, but to Norman and English eyes it might seem that, with such a height as it has, the building ought to have fully doubled its actual length. The third tower, that of a destroyed church, is worth study as an example of a striking kind of cinque-cento, the design being purely Gothic and the details being strongly Italianised. But, after all, the architectural inquirer will be best pleased with the fine Romanesque tower in the suburb of Limay, and the lover of picturesque effect will not fail to dwell on the mediæval bridge which leads thither from the town.

Limay Church, Tower, S.E.

So much for the spot, beyond the limits of his own Duchy, where William, in the words of our Chronicles, "did a rueful thing, and more ruefully it him befel." Of the points within Normandy which his name invests with their main interest, we have already spoken of his birthplace at Falaise—where the brutal work of "restoration," *i.e.* of scraping and destroying, is still going on in full force—of the field of his early victory at Val-ès-dunes, and of the victory won for him by others at Mortemer. We may, however, suggest that any one who visits Val-ès-dunes, will not do amiss if he extends his ramble as far as the churches of Cintheaux and Quilly. Cintheaux is one of the best of the small but rich twelfth-century churches which are so common in the district. And its worthy curé, the historian of Val-ès-dunes, is doing his best to bring it back to its former state, without subjecting it, like Falaise or like one of the spires of Saint Stephen's, to the cruel martyrdom of the apostle Bartholomew. Quilly is more remarkable still, as possessing a tower containing marked vestiges of that earlier Romanesque style of which Normandy contains so much fewer examples than either England or Aquitaine. Cintheaux=Centella, has also a certain historic interest in the generation after William. There, in 1105, King Henry and Duke Robert, "*duo germani fratres*," had a conference. We forget who it was who translated "*duo germani fratres*" by "two German brothers," and went on to rule that the Henry spoken of must have been the Emperor Henry the Fourth, and to remark that the conference happened not very long before his death. Cintheaux, however, has carried us from the age of William into the age of his sons, and we must retrace our steps somewhat. The sites connected with William himself will easily fall into three classes—those which belong to his wars with France and Anjou, those which figure in the Breton campaign which he waged in company with Earl Harold, and those which have a direct bearing on the Conquest of England. The second class we may easily dispose of. Of Dol and Dinan we have said somewhat already, and Dinan especially is a place familiar to many Englishmen. But we may remark that, though Dinan contains few remains of any great antiquity, few places better preserve the general effect of an ancient town. It still rises grandly above the river, spanned both by the lowly ancient bridge and the gigantic modern viaduct; the walls are nearly perfect, and houses, partly through the necessities of the site, have not spread themselves at all largely beyond them. We may add that the good sense of the inhabitants has found out a way to make excellent boulevards without sacrificing the walls to their creation. Rennes, the furthest point reached by the two comrades so soon to become enemies, is now wholly a modern city. Saint Michael's Mount has become a popular lion, which can only be seen under the vexatious companionship of a guide and a "party." It is therefore impossible to study the interior with much comfort or profit. Yet one has still time to wonder at the strange effect produced by crowding the buildings of a great monastery on the top of the rock, an effect which reaches its highest point when we go up a staircase and find ourselves landed in a cloister of singular beauty. But the rock and the buildings—nowhere better seen than from the Mount of Dol—are still there, a most striking object from every point of the landscape, Saint Michael "in peril of the sea" seeming to watch over the bay which bears his name, as from his height at Glastonbury he seems to watch over the flats and the hills peopled with the names alike of British and of West-Saxon heroes. And the vast expanse of sand brings vividly before us the scene in the Tapestry where the giant strength of the English Earl is shown lifting with ease the soldiers who found themselves engulfed in the treacherous stream.

Domfront Castle

The wars of William with Geoffrey of Anjou and Henry of Paris introduce us to several points, striking in the way both of nature and of art. Few among them surpass Domfront, William's first conquest beyond the bounds of his own Duchy, the fortress which he won by the mere terror of his name after the fearful vengeance which he had inflicted on the rebels of Alençon.[17] The spot reminds one in some degree of his own birthplace at Falaise. That is to

say, the castle crowns one rocky hill, and looks out on another, still wilder and more rugged, with a pass between them, through which runs the stream of the Varenne, a tributary of the Mayenne, as that is in its turn of the Loire. But the position of the two towns is different. Though the castle of Falaise occupies so commanding a site, the town itself is anything but one of the hill-towns, while Domfront is one of the best of the class. Not that it is the least likely to be an ancient hill-fort, like Chartres, Le Mans, or Angers; both Falaise and Domfront are, beyond all doubt, towns which have gathered round their respective castles in comparatively modern times. Both, there can be no doubt, date, in their very beginnings, from a time later than the Norman settlement. Still Domfront is practically a hill-town; the walls simply fence in the top of the height, and the town, never having reached any great size, has not yet spread itself to the bottom. A more picturesque site can hardly be found. Of the castle, the chief remnant is a shattered fragment of the keep, most likely the very fortress which surrendered to William's youthful energy.
[18] As for churches, the only one within the walls is worthless, but the church of Notre-Dame at the foot of the hill is one of the best and purest specimens of Norman work on a moderate scale to be found anywhere. The original work is nearly untouched, except that the barbarism of modern times has removed about half the nave.

Eu Church, S.E.

After Domfront had submitted to William and had become permanently incorporated with Normandy, he himself founded the fortress of Ambrières, as a border stronghold.[19] A fragment of the castle still overlooks the lower course of the Varenne, but the ground is no longer Norman. Some way further on the same road we reach Mayenne, a town whose name suggests far later warfare, but which was an important conquest of William's in the days when Maine was the border ground, and the battle-field, of Norman and Angevin. [20] The site of Mayenne, sloping, like that of Mantes, down to a large river, has caused quite another arrangement. The river is here the main point for attack and defence as well as for traffic. The castle therefore does not crown the highest point of the town, but flanks the stream with a grand range of bastions, a miniature of the mighty pile of Philip Augustus at "black Angers." This lower position of castles, thus returned to in later times, seems however to have been the usual position for the fortresses of the earliest Norman time. Before the Scandinavian conquerors were fully settled in the country, the great point was to occupy sites commanding the sea and the navigable rivers; it was a sign of quite another state of things when the lord of the soil perched himself on the crest of an inland hill. Of the earlier type of fortress we have an example in the castle of Eu, a name whose associations may seem to be wholly modern, but which is, in truth, as the border fortress of Normandy towards Flanders and the doubtful land of Ponthieu between them, one of the most historic sites in the Duchy. Eu figures prominently in the wars of Rolf; in its church William espoused his Flemish bride; in its castle he first received his renowned English guest.[21] The church of William's day has given way to a superb fabric of the thirteenth century, which needs only towers, which are strangely lacking, to rank among the finest minsters in Normandy. The castle where William and Harold met has given way to that well-known building of the House of Guise which lived to become the last home of lawful royalty in France. But the site still reminds one of the days of Rolf rather than of the days of William. It can hardly be said to command the town; it is itself commanded by higher ground immediately above it; town, church, castle, all seem from the surrounding hills to lie together in a hole. But it is admirably placed for commanding the approaches from the sea and from the low, and in Rolf's time no doubt marshy, ground lying between the town and the water. In exact contrast to Eu, stands the noble hill-castle of Arques, near Dieppe, the work of William's rebellious uncle and namesake, which he had to win by the slow process of hunger from Norman rebels and French auxiliaries.[22] The little town, with a church of later date, but of striking outline, lies low, lower than Eu; but the castle soars above it, crowning a peninsular height which forms the extremity of a long range of higher ground. The steep slopes of the hill might have seemed defence enough, but Count William did not deem his fortress secure without cutting an enormous fosse immediately within its circuit, so that any one who climbed the slope of the hill would find a deep gulf between himself and the fortress, even if he were lucky enough to escape falling headlong. The building has been greatly enlarged in later times, but the shell of Count William's keep, a huge massive square tower, is still here, as perhaps are some portions of his gateway and of his surrounding walls. The view is a noble one, and it takes in the site of that later battle of Henry of Navarre to which Arques now owes most of its renown, and which has gone some way to wipe out the memory of both Williams, Count and Duke alike.

One point more. Round the lower course of the Dive all sorts of historical associations centre. The stream divides the older and the later Normandy, but of these the later is the truer, the land where the old speech and the old spirit lingered longest. By its banks was fought the battle in which Harold Blaatand rescued Normandy from the Frank, and in which the stout Dane took captive with his own hands Lewis King of the West-Franks, the heir and partial successor of Charles.[23] There, too, are the causeway and bridge of Varaville, marking the site of the ford where William's well-timed march enabled him to strike almost as heavy a blow against the younger royalty of Paris as the Danish ally of his forefathers had struck against the elder royalty of Laon.[24] The French invaders of Normandy, King Henry at their head, had gorged themselves with the plunder of the lands west of the Dive and were now carelessly advancing towards the high ground of Auge in the direction of Lisieux. The King with his vanguard had already climbed the hill, when he looked round, only to behold the mass of his army cut to pieces before the sudden onslaught of the irresistible Duke. William had marched up from Falaise and had taken them at the right moment, almost as Harold took his Norwegian namesake at Stamford bridge. It is one of those spots where the story is legibly written on the scene. The causeway is still there, and it is easy to realise the King looking on the slaughter of his troops, and hardly withheld from rushing down to give them help which must have proved wholly in vain. The heights from which he looked down stretched to the sea, by the mouth of the river. The port of Dive, now nearly choked up with sand, was then a great haven, and there the fleet of William, assembled for the conquest of England, lay for a whole month, waiting for the favourable winds which never came till they had changed their position for the more auspicious haven of Saint Valery.

THE CÔTENTIN

1876

THE "pagus Constantinus," the peninsular land of Coutances, is, or ought to
be, the most Norman part of Normandy. Perhaps however it may be needful
first to explain that the Latin "pagus *Constantinus*" and the French *Côtentin*
are simply the same word. For we have seen a French geography-book in
which *Côtentin* was explained to mean the land of *coasts*; the peninsular
shape of the district gave it "trois côtes," and so it was called *Côtentin*. We
cannot parallel this with the derivation of Manorbeer from "man or bear";[25]
because this last is at least funny, while to derive Côtentin from *côte* is simply
stupid. But it is very like a derivation which we once saw in a Swiss
geography-book, according to which the canton of Wallis or Valais was so
called "parce que c'est la plus grande *vallée* de la Suisse." And, what is more,
a Swiss man of science, eminent in many branches of knowledge, but not
strong in etymology, thought it mere folly to call the derivation in question. It
was no good arguing when the case was as clear as the sun at noon-day. Now,
in the case of Wallis, it is certainly much easier to say what the etymology of
the name is not than to say what it is; but in the case of the Côtentin one
would have thought that it was as clear as the sun at noon-day the other way.
How did he who derived Côtentin from *côte* deal with other names of districts
following the same form? The *Bessin*, the land of Bayeux, might perhaps be
twisted into something funny, but the *Avranchin* could hardly be anything but
the district of Avranches, and this one might have given the key to the others.
But both *Côtentin* and *Bessin* illustrate a law of the geographical
nomenclature of Gaul, by which, when a city and its district bear the same
name, the name takes two slightly different forms for the city and for the
district. Thus we have Bourges and Berry, Angers and Anjou, Périgueux and
Périgord, Le Mans and Maine.[26] So *Constantia* has become Coutances; but
the adjective *Constantinus* has become Côtentin. City and district then bear
the same Imperial name as that other Constantia on the Rhine with which
Coutances is doomed to get so often confounded. How often has one seen
Geoffrey of Mowbray described as "Bishop of Constance." In an older writer
this may be a sign that, in his day, Coutances was spoken of in England as
Constance. In a modern writer this judgment of charity is hardly possible. It
really seems as if some people thought that the Conqueror was accompanied
to England by a Bishop of the city where John Huss was burned ages
afterwards.

We have called the Côtentin a peninsula, and so it is. Sir Francis Palgrave points out, with a kind of triumph, that the two Danish peninsulas, the original Jütland and this of the <u>Côtentin</u>, are the only two in Europe which point northward. And the Côtentin does look on the map very much as if it were inviting settlers from more northern parts. But the fact is that the land is not really so peninsular as it looks and as it feels. The actual projection northward from the coast of the Bessin or Calvados is not very great. It is the long coast to the west, the coast which looks out on the Norman islands, the coast which forms a right angle with the Breton coast by the Mount of Saint Michael, which really gives the land its peninsular air. We are apt to forget that the nearest coast due west of the city of Coutances does not lie in Europe. We are apt further to forget that the whole of that west coast is not Côtentin. Avranches has its district also, and the modern department of Manche takes in both, as the modern diocese of Coutances takes in the older dioceses of Coutances and Avranches.

Part of the Côtentin then is a true peninsula, a peninsula stretching out a long finger to the north-west in the shape of Cape La Hague; and this most characteristic part of the land has impressed a kind of peninsular character on the whole region. But we must not forget that the land of Coutances is not wholly peninsular, but also partly insular. The Norman islands, those fragments of the duchy which remained faithful to their natural Duke when the mainland passed under the yoke of Paris, are essential parts of the Constantine land, diocese and county. Modern arrangements have transferred their ecclesiastical allegiance to the church of Winchester, and their civil allegiance to the Empire of India; but historically those islands are that part of the land of Coutances which remained Norman while the rest stooped to become French.[27] The peninsula pointing northwards, with its neighbouring islands, save that the islands lie to the west and not to the east, might pass for no inapt figure of the northern land of the Dane. They formed a land which the Dane was, by a kind of congruity, called on to make his own. And his own he made it and thoroughly. Added to the Norman duchy by William Longsword before Normans had wholly passed into Frenchmen, with the good seed watered again by a new settlement straight from Denmark under Harold Blaatand, the Danish land of Coutances, like the Saxon land of Bayeux, was far slower than the lands beyond the Dive in putting on the speech and the outward garb of France. And no part of the Norman duchy sent forth more men or mightier, to put off that garb in the kindred, if conquered, island, and to come back to their natural selves in the form of Englishmen. The most Teutonic part of Normandy was the one part which had a real grievance to avenge on Englishmen; in their land, and in their land alone, had Englishmen, for a moment in the days of Æthelred, shown themselves as invaders and ravagers. But before the men of the Côtentin could show themselves as avengers at Senlac, they had first to be themselves overthrown at Val-ès-dunes. Before William could conquer England, he had first to conquer his own duchy by the aid of France. Bayeux and Coutances were to have no share in the spoil of York and Winchester till they had been themselves subdued by the joint might of Rouen and Paris.

It is singular enough that the two most prominent names among those which connect the Bessin and the Côtentin with England should be those of their two Bishops, Geoffrey of Mowbray, for a while Earl of Northumberland, and the more famous Odo, Bishop of Bayeux and Earl of Kent. Geoffrey would deserve a higher fame than he wins by the possession of endless manors in Domesday and by the suppression of the West-Saxon revolt at Montacute,[28] if we could believe that, according to a legend which is even now hardly exploded, the existing church of Coutances is his work. William of Durham and Roger of Salisbury would seem feeble workers in the building art beside the man who consecrated that building in the purest style of the thirteenth century in the year 1056. According to that theory, art must have been at Coutances a hundred and fifty years in advance of the rest of the world, and, after about a hundred and twenty years, the rest of the world must have begun a series of rude attempts at imitating the long-neglected model. But without attributing to the art of Coutances or the Côtentin so miraculous a development as this, the district was at all times fertile in men who could build in the styles of their several ages. A journey through the peninsula shows its scenery, so varied and in many parts so rich, adorned by a succession of great buildings worthy of the land in which they are placed. The great haven of the district is indeed more favoured by nature than by art. In the name of Cherbourg mediæval etymologists fondly saw an Imperial name yet older than that which is borne by the whole district, and the received Latin name is no other than *Cæsaris Burgus*. Yet it is far more likely that the name of Cherbourg is simply the same as our own Scarborough, and that it is so called from the rocky hills, the highest ground in the whole district, which look down on the fortified harbour, and are themselves condemned to help in its fortification. The rocks and the valley between them are worthy of some better office than to watch over an uninteresting town which has neither ancient houses to show nor yet handsome modern streets. The chief church, though not insignificant, is French and not Norman, and so teaches the wrong lesson to an Englishman who begins his Côtentin studies at this point. But, four miles or so to the west, he will find a building which is French only if we are to apply that name to what runs every chance of being præ-Norman, the work of a day when Rolf and William Longsword had not yet dismembered the French duchy. On a slight eminence overhanging the sea stands

Querqueville, with its older and its newer, its lesser and its greater, church, the two standing side by side, and with the outline of the greater—the same triapsidal form marking both—clearly suggested by the smaller. Of the smaller, which is very small indeed, one can hardly doubt that parts at least are primitive Romanesque, as old as any one chooses. It is the fellow of the little church of Montmajeur near Arles, but far ruder. But at Querqueville the name is part of the argument; the building gives its name to the place. The first syllable of Querqueville is plainly the Teutonic *kirk*; and it suggests that it got the name from this church having been left standing when most of its neighbours were destroyed in the Scandinavian inroads which created Normandy. The building has gone through several changes; the upper part of its very lofty tower is clearly a late addition, but the ground-plan, and so much of the walls as show the herring-bone work, are surely remains of a building older than the settlement of Rolf.

Valognes Church, N.E.

From the rocks of the Norman *Scarborough*, one of the only two railways which find their way into the Côtentin will carry the traveller through a district whose look, like that of so much of this side of Normandy, is thoroughly English, to Valognes, with its endless fragments of old domestic architecture, remnants of the days when Valognes was a large and aristocratic town, and with its church, where the architect has ventured, not wholly without success, on the bold experiment of giving its central parts the shape of a Gothic cupola. Is its effect improved or spoiled—it certainly is made stranger and more striking—by its grouping with a spire of late date immediately at its side? There is much to please at Valognes; but when we remember the part which the town plays in the history of the Conqueror, that it was from hence, one of his favourite dwelling-places, that he took the headlong ride which carried him away safely from the rebellious peninsula before Val-ès-dunes, we are inclined to grumble that all that now shows itself in the place itself is of far later date. The castle is clean gone; and the traveller to whom Normandy is chiefly attractive in its Norman aspect may perhaps sacrifice the Roman remains of Alleaume if the choice lies between them and a full examination of the castle and abbey of Saint Saviour on the Douve, *Saint-Sauveur-le-Vicomte*, the home of the two Neals, the centre, in the days of the second of the rebellions which caused William to ride so hard from Valognes to Rye.[29] A characteristic church or two, among them Colomby, with its long lancets, may be taken on the way; but the great object of the journey is where the little town of Saint Saviour lies on its slope, with the castle on the one hand, the abbey on the other, rising above the river at its feet. The abbey, Neal's abbey, where his monks supplanted an earlier foundation of canons, has gone through many ups and downs. Its Romanesque plan remained untouched through a great reconstruction of its upper part in the later Gothic. It fell into ruin at the Revolution, but one side of the nave and the central saddle-backed tower still stood, and now the ruin is again a perfect church, where Sisters of Mercy have replaced the monks of Saint Benedict. Here then a great part of the work of the ancient lords remains; with the castle which should be their most direct memorial the case is less clear. Besides round towers—one great one specially which some one surely must have set down as Phœnician—the great feature is the huge square tower which forms the main feature of the building, and which has thoroughly the air of a Norman keep of the eleventh or twelfth century. But when we come nearer, there is hardly a detail—round arches of course alone prove nothing—which does not suggest a later time. And the tower is attributed to Sir John Chandos, who held the castle in Edward the Third's time. Did he most ingeniously recast every detail of an elder keep, or did he choose to build exactly according to the type of an age long before his own? Anyhow, as far as general effect goes, the tower thoroughly carries us back to the days of the earlier fame of Saint Saviour. The view from its top stretches far away over the peninsula of which it was once the citadel to the backs of the hills which look down on Cherbourg and the sea, the sea which, if we believe the tale, bore the fleet of Æthelred when the elder Neal drove back English invaders more than three hundred years before Sir John Chandos.

Abbey of Lessay, S.W.

The visitor to Saint Saviour may perhaps manage to make his way straight from that place to Coutances without going back to Valognes. In any case his main object between Saint Saviour and Coutances will be the great Romanesque abbey of Lessay; only, by going back to Valognes and taking the railway to Carentan, he will be able to combine with Lessay the two very fine churches of Carentan and Periers. Of these, Carentan has considerable Romanesque portions, the arches of the central lantern and the pillars of the nave which have been ingeniously lengthened and made to bear pointed arches. Lessay, we fancy, is very little known. It is out of the way, and the country round about it, flat and dreary, is widely different from the generally rich, and often beautiful, scenery of the district. But few churches of its own class surpass it as an example of an almost untouched Norman minster, not quite of the first class in point of scale. We say untouched, because it is so practically, though a good deal of the vaulting was most ingeniously repaired after the English wars, just as Saint Stephen at Caen was after the Huguenot wars. Some miles over the *landes* bring us again into the hilly region round the episcopal city, and Coutances is seen on its hill, truly a city which cannot be hid. Of its lovely minster we once spoke in some detail;[30] of the city itself we may add that none more truly bespeaks its origin as a hill-fort. The hill is of no extraordinary height; but it is thoroughly isolated, not forming part of a

49

range like the hills of Avranches and Le Mans. And, saving the open place before the cathedral—perhaps the forum of Constantia—there is not a flat yard of ground in Coutances. The church itself is on a slope; you walk up the incline of one street and see the houses sloping down the incline of the other. In the valley on the west side of the city is a singular curiosity, several of the arches of a mediæval aqueduct.[311] Pointed arches, and buttresses against the piers, are what we are not used to in such buildings. A road by a few small churches leads to Granville on its peninsula, with its strange church where Flamboyant and *Renaissance* die away into a kind of Romanesque most unlike that of Ragusa, and the Côtentin has been gone through from north to south. The modern department and the modern diocese go on further; but the "pagus Constantinus" is now done with; the land of Avranches, the march against the Breton, has a history of its own.

THE AVRANCHIN

1876

THE town of Avranches is well known as one of those Continental spots on which Englishmen have settled down and formed a kind of little colony. A colony of this kind has two aspects in the eyes of the traveller who lights upon it. On the one hand, it is a nuisance to find one's self, on sitting down to a *table-d'hôte* in a foreign town, in the middle of ordinary English chatter. Full of the particular part of the world in which he is, the traveller may hear all parts of the world discussed from some purely personal or professional aspect, without a single original observation to add anything to his stock of ideas. On the other hand, it must be allowed that the presence of an English settlement anywhere always brings with it a degree of civilisation in many points such as is not always found in towns of much greater size which our countrymen do not frequent. But to the historical traveller Avranches is almost dead. A few stones heaped together are all that remains of the cathedral, and another stone marks the sight of the north door where Henry the Second received absolution for his share in the murder of Thomas. The city which formed the halting-place of Lanfranc on his way from Pavia to Bec is now chiefly to be noticed for its splendid site, and as a convenient starting-point for other places where more has been spared. Avranches, like Coutances, is a hill-city, and, as regards actual elevation, it is even more of a hill-city than Coutances. But then the hill of Coutances is an isolated hill, while Avranches stands on the projecting bluff of a range. Seen from the sands of Saint Michael's Bay, the site proclaims itself as one which, before the fall of its chief ornament, must have been glorious beyond words. It might have been Laon, as it were, with, at favourable tides at least, the estuary washing the foot of its hill. What the view is from the height itself is implied in what has just been said. The bay, with the consecrated Mount and the smaller Tombelaine by its side, the Breton coast stretching far away, the Mount of Dol coming, perhaps within the range of sight, certainly within the range of ideas, the goodly land on either side of the city, the woods, the fields —for in the Avranchin we are still in a land of pasture and hedgerows—all tell us that it was no despicable heritage of his own to which Hugh of Avranches added his palatine earldom of Chester. And if Avranches gave a lord to one great district of England, England presently gave a lord to Avranches. The Avranchin formed part of the fief of the Ætheling Henry, the fief so often lost and won again, but where men had at least some moments of order under the stern rule of the Lion of Justice, while the rest of Normandy

51

in the days of Robert was torn in pieces by the feuds of rival lords and countesses. But musings of this kind would be more to the point if the city itself had something more to show than a tower or two of no particular importance—if, in short, the hill of Avranches was crowned by such a diadem of spires and cupolas as the hill of Coutances. As it is, Avranches is less attractive in itself than it is as the best point for several excursions in the Avranchin land. The excursion to the famous Mount of Saint Michael and its fortified abbey need not here be dwelled on. No one can walk five minutes in the streets of Avranches without being reminded that the city is the starting-place for "le mont Saint-Michel." But no one suggests a visit to Saint James nor even to Mortain and its waterfalls. Nor should we ourselves suggest a visit to Saint James, except to those who may be satisfied with a beautiful bit of natural scenery, heightened by the thought that the spot is directly connected with the memory of William, indirectly with that of Harold.

When we write "Saint James," we are not translating.[32] The "castrum sancti Jacobi" appears as "Saint James" in Wace, and it is "Saint James" to this day alike in speech and in writing. The fact is worthy of some notice in the puzzling history of the various forms of the apostolic names Jacobus and Johannes and their diminutives. *Jacques* and *Jack* must surely be the same; how then came *Jack* to be the diminutive of *John*? Anyhow this Norman fortress bears the name of the Saint of Compostela in a form chiefly familiar in Britain and Aragon, though it is not without a cognate in the Italian *Giacomo*. The English forms of apostolic names are sometimes borne even now by Romance-speaking owners, as M. James Fazy and M. John Lemoinne bear witness. But here the name is far too old for any imitative process of this kind. And it is only as applied to the place itself that the form "James"[33] is used; the inn is the "Hôtel Saint-Jacques," and "Saint-Jacques" is the acknowledged patron of the parish. Anyhow the effect is to give the name of the place an unexpectedly English air. Perhaps such an air is not wholly out of place in the name of a spot which was fortified against the Breton by a prince who was to become King of the English, and whose fortification led to a war in which two future and rival Kings of the English fought side by side.

For the castle of Saint James was one of the fortresses raised by William's policy to strengthen the Norman frontier against the *Bret-Welsh* of Gaul, just as in after days he and his Earls raised fortresses on English ground to strengthen the English frontier against the *Bret-Welsh* of Britain. It stands very near to the border, and we can well understand how its building might give offence to the Breton Count Conan, and so lead to the war in which William and Harold marched together across the sands which surround the consecrated Mount. In this way Saint James plays an indirect part in English history, and it plays another when it was one of the first points of his lost territory to be won back by Henry the Ætheling after his brothers had driven him out of the Mount and all else that he had.[34] But the place keeps hardly anything but its memories and the natural beauty of its site. A steep peninsular hill looks down on a narrow and wooded valley with a *beck*—that is the right word in the land which contains Caude*bec* and *Bec* Herlouin—running round its base. The church—a strange modern building with some ancient portions used up again —stands on the extreme point of the promontory. This seems the best point for commanding the whole valley, and we may perhaps guess that a less devout prince than William would not have scrupled to raise his donjon at least within the consecrated precinct. But he chose the southern side of the hill, the side to be sure most directly looking towards the enemy; and church and castle stood side by side on the hill without interfering with each other. But the visitor to Saint James—if Saint James should ever get any visitors— must take care not to ask for the *château*. If he does, he will be sent to the other side of the valley, to a modern house, on a lovely site certainly, and working in some portions of mediæval work, but which has nothing to do with the castle of the Conqueror. The name for that, so far as it keeps a name, is "le *fort*." The open space by the church is the "place du Fort," and the inquirer will soon find that on the south the hill-side is scarped and strengthened by a wall. That is all that is left of the castle of Saint James; but it is enough to call up memories of days which, from an English as well as from a local point of view, are worth remembering.

COUTANCES AND SAINT-LO

1891

GEOFFREY OF MOWBRAY, Bishop of Coutances, appears once in Domesday as Bishop of Saint-Lo, but it must not therefore be thought that he had his bishopstool in the town so called, or that the great church of Saint-Lo was ever the spiritual head of the peninsular land of Coutances. There is indeed every opportunity for confusion on the subject. The Bishops of Coutances were lords of Saint-Lo in the present department of La Manche; but, so far as they were Bishops of Saint-Lo at all, it was of quite another Saint-Lo, namely, of a church so called in the city of Rouen. There, when the Côtentin was over-run by the still heathen Northmen, the Bishops of Coutances took refuge, carrying with them Saint-Lo himself—*Sanctus Laudus*, a predecessor in the bishopric—in the form of his relics. When heathen Northmen were turned into Christian Normans, the Bishops of Coutances went home again, but the title which they had picked up on their travels seems to have stuck to them. As they had to do with two things, both called Saint-Lo, as well as with their own city, the error of speech was not wonderful. But, setting aside times of havoc, when there was nothing left to be head of, Coutances always remained the formal head, ecclesiastical and civil, of the Côtentin, the "pagus Constantinus," which took its name from the city. The town of Saint-Lo has now outstripped Coutances in the matter of temporal honour as the head of the department of La Manche, though that dignity was not assigned to it without a good deal of opposition on the part of the elder seat of rule. The same series of changes gave to ecclesiastical Coutances, if not a higher dignity, at least a wider jurisdiction. When the episcopal church of Coutances, after being put to various strange uses in the revolutionary time, became once more a place of Christian worship and the head church of the diocese, that diocese was enlarged by the ecclesiastical territory of Avranches. Avranches and Lisieux have both vanished from the roll of the six suffragans of the Archbishop of Rouen, Primate of Normandy. But Avranches has suffered worse things than Lisieux. The Lexovian bishopstool has passed away; but the church that held it is still there. From Avranches the church itself has vanished. It is from its site only that we look down on the wide plain at our foot, on the Mount of the Archangel in its bay, and the rocks of Cancale beyond.[35]

There is no need to describe anew a building so well known as the cathedral church of Coutances. There is no need to argue against, there is hardly need to wonder at, the strange belief against which Gally Knight and others had to fight, that this beautiful example of the fully developed Early Gothic was really the work of that Bishop Geoffrey who blessed the Norman host on its march from Hastings to Senlac.[36] That belief was indeed a strange one. It implied that some nameless genius at Coutances had, in the middle of the eleventh century, suddenly, at a blow, invented the fully developed style of the thirteenth—that this great discovery was kept hidden at Coutances till the very end of the twelfth—that then various people in Normandy, France, England, and above all Saint Hugh of Burgundy, began to make many, and at first not very successful, attempts to imitate what the men of one spot in the Côtentin had known, and must have been proud of, for a century and a half. The local invention of Perpendicular at Gloucester, and its spreading abroad by the great Bishops of Winchester forty or fifty years later, is a remarkable fact; but it is a small matter to this fiction. So strange a vagary need no longer be discussed; but it is worthy of a place in the memory among odd delusions. As an honest delusion, it is at least more respectable than making Alfred found things at Oxford and Ripon.

Notre-Dame, Saint-Lo, S.E.

In position, Saint-Lo, town and church, outdoes Coutances. It is, we believe, a favourite resort of artists, and it deserves to be so. At Coutances we are on a hill. If we draw near to it by railway, we see the three towers of the cathedral church soaring far above us, and even the two towers of Saint Peter are by no means on our own level. The town stands on a height, at the end of a range of high ground; yet somehow there is not the same feeling of a hill town about Coutances which there is in many other places—one thing perhaps is that there is no river. The hill of Coutances is not a hill simply rising from a plain; there are valleys on two sides, and we ask for a stream at the bottom of them as naturally as we do at Edinburgh. At Saint-Lo, the Vire, with the rocky hill rising high above it, is the chief feature of the landscape. And as we pass by on the railway and look up, the two graceful spires of the church of Our Lady seem quite worthy of their position. We feel at once that the characteristic feature of Normandy and England, the central tower, is missing. But, accepting a French effect instead of a Norman one, the impression made by Saint-Lo and its church is a very striking one. We must go on to Coutances and come back to Saint-Lo, and then walk along the banks of the Vire if we wish to take in the fact, that even the spires of Saint-Lo, much less the church as a whole, have no claim to belong to the same class of buildings as Coutances. In neither case is the church built, as that of Avranches must have been, like Durham, on the brow of the hill. There is a considerable space, at Saint-Lo a busy market, between the west front and the steep. From any point in this space the effect of the west front of Saint-Lo is striking beyond its actual size. The towers are of different dates, and do not altogether match, which has the effect of thrusting the central door rather out of its place. But the front is a grand one all the same. One must go down below, and see from how many points the towers, and even the spires, are lost among the houses, before we find out how comparatively small they are. And in the body of the church we see a marked example of an opportunity thrown away. That the church is much smaller than that of Coutances is a fact of less importance than it would be in England. A characteristic of French architecture is the constant reproduction of the designs of great churches on a much smaller scale. This is a thing which we know nothing of in England, where the parish church and the minster are buildings of two different types, each of which may be equally good in its own way. The church of Saint Peter at Coutances, much smaller than that of Saint-Lo, will illustrate this position. And there are plenty of instances, from graceful miniatures like Norrey and Les Petits Andelys up to churches of considerable size. But at Saint-Lo, whatever little outline the church has apart from its spires it gets from a series of gables along the aisles, something like those of Saint Giles at Oxford. Inside we have a not very successful *hallenkirche*, three bodies without a clerestory, Bristol-fashion. Much of the work is good enough of its kind, and the late stained glass is worth studying; but, as soon as we leave the west front behind there is a strange lack of design in the whole building, inside and out.

But Notre-Dame is not the only church at Saint-Lo. Both De Caumont and Gally Knight have a good deal to tell us about the church of Saint Cross, which it seems that some antiquaries had carried back to the days of Charles the Great. *Distinguendum est.* To carry back a piece of Romanesque of any date to a date too early, but still within Romanesque times, is a mistake of quite another kind from attributing finished work of the thirteenth century to Geoffrey of Mowbray in the eleventh. Gally Knight himself erred more slightly in the same way. He knew very well that the work at Saint Cross could not be of the eighth century; but he took it for the eleventh instead of the twelfth. No one can blame him for that at the time when he wrote. But both Gally Knight and De Caumont saw some things at Saint Cross which are not to be seen now, and some things are to be seen now which they did not see. They saw a twelfth-century church which had gone through some changes and additions, and they also saw some considerable monastic buildings, of part of which, a vault with what seems to be a rather classical column, De Caumont gives a drawing. Here it is, if anywhere, that one would look for the earlier date of Romanesque. But all outside the church itself has perished. The church itself has, since De Caumont's visit, been greatly enlarged in imitation of the twelfth-century work, and the twelfth-century work itself has been frightfully scraped and scored after the manner of restoration. Still several bays of arcade and triforium are left in such a state that we can see the original design of round arches with Norman mouldings on piers with shafts with foliated caps. The church, before it was pulled about, must have been a fine one, but assuredly of the twelfth century and not of any earlier time.

One bit of detail which Gally Knight saw may still be seen untouched. "The west entrance," he says, "is barbarously adorned with a grotesque group, in high relief, which represents the Subjugation of the Evil Spirit." The power subjugated takes the shape of a creature, said to be a toad, with his head downwards. The work of subjugation is done by two men below pulling at his head with ropes.

Though Romanesque is the thing which one wishes most to see, yet a church in such a case as Saint Cross at Saint-Lo teaches one less than the smaller churches at Coutances. Both of these, Saint Peter and Saint Nicolas, aim at reproducing on a smaller scale the most distinctive feature of the episcopal church. This is the grand central octagon, with its *quasi*-domical treatment inside. But in both of the smaller churches it is coupled with a single western tower. This arrangement of a central and western tower is rare in England, because in most of the cases where it once existed one or other of the towers has fallen down. In France it is somewhat more usual, and in Auvergne it is the rule. Here at Saint Peter's a vast deal of effective and stately outline is crowded into a wonderfully small space on the ground. The two towers, tall and massive, rise with a strangely small allowance of nave between them. Begun in the latest Gothic, carried out in early *Renaissance*, their outline is rich but fantastic, and in many points of general view the three towers of the cathedral do not despise the two of Saint Peter's as fellows in a most effective piece of grouping. The internal effect, which the height might have made very striking, is not equal to the external outline. The discontinuous impost, the ugliest invention of French Flamboyant, may perhaps be endured in some subordinate place; it is intolerable in the main piers of a church. The treatment of the central tower within is very curious; the lantern of the cathedral is here translated into an Italianising style. In short we have here, as we have seen in many places, specially at Troyes,[37] as we shall see again in a most marked form at Argentan, that curious process of transition from mediæval to *Renaissance* detail which in England we are familiar with in houses, but which in France is to be largely studied in churches also. At Saint Nicolas, though the building is later in date and less striking in design, such work as keeps any style at all is better. Its nave is free from discontinuous imposts.

Lastly, at Coutances the mediæval aqueduct, a little way out of the town, must not be forgotten. There are not many such anywhere, save one or two in Sicily. It is a pity that of late years the ivy has been allowed to grow over the arches to that degree that a new-comer would hardly know whether they were round or pointed.

St. Nicolas, Coutances, Interior

HAUTEVILLE-LA-GUICHARD

1891

THE experienced antiquarian traveller is perfectly familiar with the doctrine that in many cases it is more satisfactory to find a mere site than to find anything on the site. Suppose one is castle-stalking in Maine, suppose one is looking for primæval walls in the Volscian or the Hernican land. If one does not find the exact thing that one wishes, the second-best luck is to find the place where it once was, and to find nothing there. Best of all is to find a fortress of the right age on its mound surrounded by its ditch; next to this is to find the mound surrounded by its ditch, but supporting nothing at all. If there is nothing at all, there is nothing that stands in our way, whereas anything of a later date does stand in our way. But what are we to say when we cannot even find the site, and when the name seems meant for some other place than that to which maps and common fame attach it? So it is with what would be, if we could only find it, one of the most memorable sites, in its own way of being memorable, to be found in all Western Normandy. We say in its own way of being memorable, because, even if we found ditch and mound and tower all as they should be, their claim to historic reverence would not be that they themselves were the witnesses of any specially memorable acts. Its sound has gone forth into all lands; but it is in lands far away from the site that we seek that the deeds were wrought which made the name of the site famous. We are at Coutances; we seek for Hauteville. The Hauteville that we seek is not that which seems to occur most naturally to the mind of Coutances. It is not Hauteville-*sur-mer*; it is the namesake that bears the speaking surname of Hauteville-*la-Guichard*. We seek, in short, for the home of Tancred and his sons. Their statues are now again set up in their niches on the north side of the church of Coutances. But the artist has surely given William of the Iron Arm far too mild a look. It is true that he and all the rest are tricked out as shepherds of the people, in royal, or at least ducal, apparel. It may be then that even he of the Iron Arm, when thus attired, ought not to look as one fancies he must have looked when he sailed into the haven of Syracuse as the brother-in-arms of George Maniakês and Harold Hardrada.

As an episode in the history of the world, one is tempted to think that the fellowship of three such warriors as those, each representing the tongue, the speech, and the mode of warfare of his own folk, is the most striking scene in the whole story of the house of Hauteville. But it is naturally the brother whose deeds have had more abiding results who has made the deepest impression on the minds of men, and who has stamped his surname on the place of his birth. One might almost have been better pleased if Hauteville were known as the Hauteville of Tancred himself rather than by the name of any of his sons. But, if it was to bear the name of one of his sons, one cannot wonder at the son who was chosen. Hauteville is Hauteville-*la-Guichard*, the Hauteville of Robert the *Wiscard*, him whom Palermo knows in one character and Rome in another. A good deal of local history lies hid in these surnames of places. The place took the name of its lord to distinguish it from other places of the same name. But we cannot always say why it took the name of this or that particular lord, that is, in effect, why it took its name in this or that particular generation. Old Roger of Beaumont, who stayed to look after Normandy and its duchess while Duke William went to seek a crown in England, is so distinctly Roger of Beaumont that it seems only fair that his Beaumont should be known back again as the Beaumont of Roger.[38] His sons are of Meulan, of Leicester, of Warwick, rather than of Beaumont. Beaumont-*le-Roger* is felt at once to be the becoming name of his home. Nearer to Hauteville, Saint-Jean, between Avranches and Granville, cradle of all who have written themselves *de sancto Iohanne*, is Saint-Jean-*le-Thomas*, after Thomas, its lord in the days of Henry the First. His name is written in Orderic, but he is hardly so famous even as the name-father of Beaumont, much less as the name-father of Hauteville. One needs to know the exact state of things at Saint-Jean in the days of Thomas, before one can tell why the place took his name as its surname rather than the name of any other lord before or after. But mark that it was the Christian name only that Saint-Jean could take; it could not, like *La Lande-Patry* and *Longueville-Giffart*, take the surname of the house which was called after itself. But if Hauteville had to take the name of a Tancreding, Robert was the obvious one to choose, and his surname of the *Wiscard* was the most distinctive name that the family could show. The fame of Robert, the actual founder of the Apulian duchy and indirectly of the Sicilian kingdom, the ally of Gregory the Seventh, the deliverer or the destroyer of Rome, the invader of Eastern Europe, must have quite overshadowed the fame of his elder brothers. And, while he lived, it must have overshadowed the fame of Roger of Sicily also.[39] The Great Count was the younger brother and the liegeman of the Duke. It was later events which caused the youngest branch of the house of Hauteville to outstrip all that had gone before it, to rise in the next generation to the royal crown of Sicily, and in the female line to the crown of Jerusalem and the crown of Rome.

It is then the Hauteville of Robert Wiscard, Hauteville-la-Guichard, that we seek for. As far as the map goes, as far as the road goes, there is no difficulty. But it is a strange thing that in such books as we are able to carry with us we can find no account of Hauteville whatever. Joanne does not mention it; Murray does not mention it; it does not come within the range of De Caumont's *Statistique Routière de la Basse Normandie*. A little local book on Coutances and its neighbourhood looks upon Hauteville either as too far off or unworthy of notice. Yet the distance at least, as the map witnesses, is not frightful, and one would have thought that the mere fact of the setting up of the new statues would have awakened the writer of the Coutances guidebook to the fact that such a spot was not far off. Anyhow, if all refuse to describe, the place seems to describe itself. *Hauteville, Alta Villa*, must surely be what its name implies. We may have unluckily forgotten the warning of Geoffrey Malaterra that Hauteville was not so much called from the height of any hill ("non quidem tantum pro excellentia alicuius montis in quo sita sit"), but rather prophetically, from the height of power and glory to which men who went from it should climb ("sed quoniam, ut credimus, aliquo auspicio ad considerationem praenotantis eventum et prosperos successus eiusdem villae futurorum haeredum, Dei adiutorio et sua presenuitate gradatim altioris honoris culmen scandentium"). We look then for a high place. It might be bold to expect to see the high place crowned by any actual building of the days of Tancred; but it seems only reasonable to argue that Hauteville must be *Hauteville*, that it must stand high. We feel sure of finding, perhaps, if our hopes are very daring, the eagle's nest on the top of the rock, or perhaps, what in Norman scenery is far more likely, the mound, natural or artificial, with its ditches, rivals, it may be, of Arques. And, where there is so little chance of finding any building of Tancred's own day, we cherish the hope that the site of his dwelling may stand wholly void, and may not have been turned to support any other building of later times.

In this fairly hopeful frame of mind, we set forth from Coutances to the north-east. The path at least is easy enough. After some miles of *route nationale*, with a fine view of the towers of Coutances for those who look backwards, we turn off into a *route départementale*. And all who are used to French roads know well that a *route nationale* is always excellent, and that a *route départementale* is always endurable and something more. We have one or two gentle ups and downs; but we neither see nor feel anything to suggest the presence or the neighbourhood of an *alta villa*. Presently a gentle down rather than a gentle up brings us to a small village, a church with a good example of the usual saddle-back tower, and with a few houses around it. We are told, and the ordnance map confirms the statement, that this is Hauteville, Hauteville-la-Guichard. Here then is the home of the Norman gentleman of the twelfth century, whose sons grew into counts and dukes in the southern lands, and whose remoter descendants wore the crowns of kingship and of Empire. With this knowledge, we are staggered to find ourselves, if not actually in a hole, yet in something much nearer to a hole than to a height, in a spot which, of the two, would seem to be more fittingly called *Basseville* than *Haute*. A slightly rising ground to the east of the church kindles again some faint hopes, the more so when the bystanders, again confirmed by the map, point out this direction as the way to the *château*. But *château*, in modern French use, is a dangerous word, and even the higher ground did not at all answer our preconceived notion of Hauteville. Still, not to throw away the faintest chance, we go on in the direction pointed out, trusting to our natural wits, for we had nothing else to guide us. Our books had failed us; nor did we, as sometimes happens, light on some intelligent priest or other person more likely to help us than the ordinary villager. A short further drive through two or three narrower roads and their turnings brings us to a spot beyond which there is clearly nothing "carossable" or even "jackassable." We come to two ranges of buildings standing among fields, buildings which have greatly gone down in the world, but which proclaim themselves as the remains of a *château* in the later French sense, or perhaps only of its outhouses. The modern *château* does indeed often enough stand on the site of the ancient *castle*; but here were no signs whatever of mound or ditch, though we ran into several fields to look for them. And, though we were certainly on higher ground than the church and village, there was nothing at all to suggest why the name of the place should have been called Hauteville.

The only hope now is to go back to the village, on the chance either of finding out something more by the light of nature or of lighting on some one who can tell us something. To the south of the church, as to the east, there is some ground rather higher than the village itself; but we see nothing of a mound, nothing to suggest an *alta villa*. But some farm-buildings to the west of the church attract the eye; they are not of yesterday; a round tower, seemingly belonging to a gateway, suggests a *château* which has taken the place of a *château-fort*. And, hard by, some of our company are led, perhaps by their noses, to an undoubted ditch, though not exactly a fellow of Arques, Marsala, or Old Sarum. And it is more than a common ditch; it is deep; it is four-sided, and it fences in a distinct plot of ground. Our thoughts have come down so low from the lofty donjon with the vision of which we set out that we begin to think of the smaller kind of moated houses in our own land. The rectory at Slymbridge in Gloucestershire had, some years back at least, a moat round it. Some traces of a moat were not long ago still to be seen at the Bishop's court-house at Wookey in Somerset. Is it possible that this unsavoury ditch really marks out the home precinct of the father of kings? Can it be that Tancred lived within it, perhaps in a wooden house, defended by a palisade and by such a ditch? We do not like the guess, but we have no better, and it really is not so absurd as it sounds. We must remember that, in Tancred's day, at least in Tancred's youth, the existence of stone castles is a little problematical. It is certain that there are few or none left of so early a date; but Normandy has seen so many seasons of the destruction of castles that it is rash to say positively that there never were any. In Tancred's day and later we often hear of the "*domus defensabilis*," as distinguished from the castle. And, as the famous one at Brionne, which so long defied the arms of Duke William, is defined as "*aula lapidea*,"[40] it seems implied that a "*domus defensabilis*" might be only "*lignea*." To be sure the stone house at Brionne had in the river Rille a ready-made moat in every way better than the ditch that we have stumbled on at Hauteville. In England, at the same time, we should have been perfectly satisfied with a wooden "aula" as the dwelling place of a powerful thegn, but then we should have looked for it on something of a mound, like the home of Wiggod at Wallingford. Certainly, a frightfully stinking ditch of no great width, compassing a square field, is a poor find after the hopes with which we set out. But, in the absence of all help from books or men, it is all that we have to offer. We should be glad if anybody would tell us of something better; but this is all we could make out for ourselves. The name is hardly a greater difficulty on this lower site than on the higher ground of the *château*. It may be then—we hope it is not so, but it may be—that it was within this ditch that Humphrey and Drogo and William of the Iron Arm were so carefully brought up by their good stepmother, that it was here that the Wiscard played his first childish tricks, with the yet smaller Roger as a willing younger brother. Tancred's estate, we are told, was not large enough to feed his two batches of children; that was the reason why they went to seek their fortunes so far off. If they had stayed at home, the estate might possibly have grown; for we are told by their own biographer that it was the nature of the sons of Tancred, when they saw that anybody else had anything, to take it to themselves. Perhaps this dangerous tendency extended only to misbelievers, schismatics, or at least men of other tongues. Otherwise such vigorous annexers of other men's lands might have found more than one chance at home, in days of confusion, of enlarging the estate of Hauteville. In short we may speculate on many matters; we can only say what we have seen and what we have not. And at the last moment a frightful thought comes upon us. We have with us one book of Gally Knight's, but it is only the Norman book. But he wrote another book, in which the house of Hauteville plays a great part. What if he went to Hauteville and found out all about it and put it all in print, only not in his Norman, but in his Sicilian book.

MORTAIN AND ITS SURROUNDINGS

1892

IN the course either of a Norman journey or of any study of Norman matters, the thought is constantly suggesting itself that there is an important class of people who are always using the names of the places through which we go, but who seem to attach no meaning to them. The whole tribe of genealogists, local antiquaries, and the like, are, in the nature of things, constantly speaking of Norman places, or at least of the families which take their names from them. But it never seems to come into their heads that these places are real places still in being on the face of the earth. What was the state of mind of the endless people who have spoken of both King Stephen and King John in earlier stages of being by the strange title of "Earl of Moreton"? Do they think they took their title from Moreton-in-the-Marsh, or do they mix those kings up with the Earl of Moreton in Scotland, who died by the maiden a good while later? And, if they try to improve their spelling, and to give it more of a continental look, perhaps he comes out in some such shape as "Count of Mortaigne." That is to say, no distinction is made between *Mortain*, *Moretolium* or *Moretonium*, in the Avranchin, and *Mortagne*, *Mauritania*, in Perche. Yet the two towns are both there, each in its old place, though in official speech we have no longer to speak of the Avranchin, but of the department of La Manche, no longer of Perche, but of the department of Orne. There are railways, branch railways certainly, which lead to both; there is no difficulty in getting to either, and Mortain at least, the one most closely connected with our own history, is very well worth going to indeed.

The position of Mortain, to say nothing else, is certainly one of the most beautiful to be found in any region which does not aspire to the sublimity of mountain scenery. The waterfalls have been famous ever since Sir Francis Palgrave connected them with the story of the place and its counts. But the whole position of town, castle, everything about Mortain, is lovely. The town itself in a strange way suggests Taormina. It stands in somewhat the same sort on a kind of ledge on a hill-side, with higher hills rising behind it. But while Taormina looks straight down on the Ionian Sea, Mortain looks down only on the narrow dale of the little river Cance, with its steep banks rising on the other side. Yet there are spots among the limestone rocks which rise about and above Mortain which call up other Sicilian memories. If the traveller intrusts himself to the care of a local guide he will certainly be carried to the little chapel of Saint Michael overhanging the town. From that height he will be rewarded by a wide view, the most part of which, over the rich Norman plain, is as unlike Sicily as may be. But, on another side, the greater Mount of the Archangel may be seen far away floating on its bay, and the position of the chapel itself—old, but modernised and no great work of art—called up for a moment that chapel of Saint Blaise on the Akragantine rocks, which once was the temple of Dêmêtêr and her Child. And, if one only had the means of finding out, it may be that the Archangel displaced some Celtic powers, such as those which Gregory of Tours still knew as abiding on the Puy de Dôme of Auvergne. But the life of Mortain as Mortain is, or rather as Mortain, with its counts and its canons, once was, began at a lower point, at a point lower than the town itself. The Moretolian akropolis, like some others, was not an akropolis in the literal sense, for the good reason that the point of most value for military purposes was not the most lofty. The windings of the little stream allow of the projection of a bold peninsular rock, joined by a kind of isthmus to the main hill on which the town stands. Here stood the castle; town and church rise above it, and higher hills rise above town and church. But no higher point was so well suited for the purposes of a great and strong fortress. On that spot therefore the castle of Mortain arose; the town, the church, the suburb on the opposite height with its smaller church, the house of nuns above the waterfalls, the Archangel's chapel on the highest point of all, were alike satellites of the castle. They came into being, because the castle had come into being. Count Robert, the brother of the Conqueror, founded the great church of Mortain; but he founded it only because some one before him had founded the castle.

The castle is gone; a few pieces of wall on the rock are all that remains. Mortain is now ruled, not by a count, but by a sub-prefect, and the sub-prefect has made his home on the site of the home of the count. The sub-prefect of Mortain is therefore in one sort to be envied above all sub-prefects, and even prefects too. Such functionaries are commonly quartered in some dull spot in the middle of a town. The sub-prefect of Mortain dwells, and doubtless goes through the duties of his sub-prefecture, in a fair house in a fair garden. That house is the *château* that is, on the site of the *château-fort* that was, looking down on the valley, looking up at the hills, looking across at the church which marks the hermitage of the Blessed Vital. Whether from any point he can actually look over on the lesser waterfall, one must be the sub-prefect or his guest to know. Such is the change, and perhaps one should not regret it; a sub-prefect is certainly a more peaceful representative of authority than a mediæval count. But he is less picturesque and less ancient; and his dwelling follows the pattern of its inhabitant. Sub-prefects are a fruit of the principles of 1789, and it would doubtless be easy to find out who was the first of the sub-prefects of Mortain. Nor is it hard to find out who was the first of the counts. We came upon him in Malger, son of Duke Richard the Fearless. But we are tempted to think that the first of the counts of Mortain need not have been absolutely the first man to make himself a stronghold on the peninsula rock of Mortain, whether for his own defence or for the better harrying of his neighbours.

From Count Malger the castle of Mortain, and all that went with the castle of Mortain, passed to his son William the Warling.[41] Such seems to be the obvious English shape of *Warlencus*; but we have a natural curiosity to know what a *Warling* is, and why William was so called. The name has an attractive sound, and some have seen in it that same approach to a *warlock* which Gibbon saw to a *wiseacre* in the surname of Robert Wiscard. We have also a natural curiosity to know whether Duke William really had any good reason for banishing him, and thereby giving the Wiscard another comrade in the Apulian wars. We care more for the reputation of William the Great than for that of William the Warling: the accuser of the Warling too was the first recorded Bigod.[42] That is, he was the first who bore that name as a surname; for Normans in general were scoffed at by Frenchmen as *bigods*, *bigots*,— never mind the spelling or the meaning—and also as drinkers of beer. We have that reverence for a much later Bigod that we had rather not think that any Bigod told lies; but there is an awkward oath which an intermediate Bigod took at the time of the election of Stephen. So we will not venture to go beyond the fact that Duke William gave the lands of the Warling to his half-brother Robert. We know him on Senlac; we know him in Cornwall; we know him through all the western lands; we know him most of all on that Montacute of his founding which once was Leodgaresburh, scene of the Invention of the Holy Cross of Waltham.[43]

The West-Saxon knew Count Robert only as a spoiler, the Norman of Mortain knew him as a great ecclesiastical founder. In 1082 he founded the collegiate church of Saint Evroul "in castro Moretonii" for a Dean and eight Canons, to whom seven more were added by other benefactors. He also built or rebuilt the church, and, just as in the case of Harold at Waltham, the language of the charter seems to imply that he built the church first and then founded the canons to serve in it. There was a time—it seems not so very long ago—when Gally Knight had to fight against people who believed that the present church was of Count Robert's own building. So to believe was indeed one degree less grotesque than to believe that the far more advanced church of Coutances was earlier still. Gally Knight easily saw that there was nothing in the church which could be of Count Robert's time except the fine Romanesque doorway on the south side. And even that we should now call too advanced for Count Robert's own work; we should set it down for the last finish of a building which doubtless took some time to make complete in all its parts.

It is common enough in England to find a grand doorway of the twelfth century left in a church where everything else has been rebuilt. Later builders clearly admired them and spared them. Much more would this be the case at Mortain, where the building of the new church must have begun no very long time after the adding of this last finish to the old. The style of the building is Transition, and advanced Transition; it is all but early Gothic. The pointed arch alone is used; the only trace of Romanesque feeling is to be seen in the short columns of the arcade, and in the extreme simplicity of the triforium and clerestory, a single unadorned lancet in each. The vaulting is naturally a little later; that at least, with the English-looking shafts from which it springs, is in the fully developed Pointed style.

The plan of the church of Saint Evroul, Mortain, is as simple as a church that has aisles can be. We were going to say that it is a perfect basilica; but no; the basilica commonly has the transepts and the arch of triumph. At Mortain the same simple arcade runs round nave, choir, and apse without break of any kind. Within the building the effect of this austere and untouched simplicity— no one at Mortain has altered a window or added a chapel—is perfectly satisfactory. Many buildings are larger and more enriched; not many can be said to be more perfect wholes. Save in the matter of multiplied aisles within and flying buttresses without, Mortain may pass for Bourges in small. And, just as at Bourges, the external outline is less satisfactory than the internal effect. A single body of this kind has in itself no outline at all; it depends on its tower or towers. At Mortain the usual central tower of a great Norman church could not be; but neither has Saint Evroul the two Western towers of Saint-Lo and Séez; the arrangement designed was rather a development of the side towers common in the smaller churches of the district. A tower on each side was designed and begun. They stand near the east end; but they are not eastern towers like those of Geneva and many German churches. They stand outside the aisles, so as not to interrupt the continuous design within. They therefore do not really group with the apse; they are detached towers whose lowest stage just touches that of the church. But we are speaking as if both towers were there. In truth only the southern one was carried up, and that only to a height very little above the ridge of the roof, and there furnished with a saddle-back. Such a tower lends the building hardly any increase of outline in the distance, and in a near view it is chiefly remarkable for the oddness of the wonderfully long coupled windows on the west side, which are not continued all round. Save only the simple and graceful west front and the general goodness of the design and execution, the beauties of the church of Mortain are certainly to be sought within.

The castle looks up at the church, which stands on the rather steep slope of the hill, the effect of which is that the east end can hardly be seen, except from a considerable distance. Above it is the *hospice*, with the fragment of a church with a saddle-back to its central tower. Above again is the chapel of Saint Michael. Of quite another value from Saint Michael is a church a little way out of Mortain, in the near neighbourhood of the waterfalls, with rocks above it and rocks below. This is the church of nuns known as *l'Abbaye Blanche*, a foundation of Count William of Mortain in 1105. As the next year he was taken at Tinchebray and kept in prison for the rest of his days, he was not likely to do much in the way of building. The church described long ago by Gally Knight and De Caumont is palpably later than his day. It is of the Transition, and it is a much less advanced example of the Transition than the church of Mortain. Whatever Count William meant to found, the actual house was Cistercian, and the church carries Cistercian severity to its extremest point. One thinks of Kirkstall; but Kirkstall, plain as it is, drew majesty from its grand and simple outline; the White Abbey is small; it has, through the lack of a central tower, no outline without, and its small scale hinders the effect of Kirkstall.[44] One might even say that, in buildings of this class—not in those of more elaborate design—something is gained, as with the monuments of Rome, by being somewhat out of repair. Anyhow, in connexion with Mortain, the White Abbey does not lack architectural importance. It is very odd if anybody took the collegiate church to be the older. The White Abbey is a truly Cistercian building, a simple cross with a flat east end, no aisles to the nave, but chapels east of the transepts. It follows the usual law of Transitional buildings. The main constructive arches are pointed; the windows are round-headed in the eastern part, pointed in the western. The cloister and chapter-house have round arches; the remains of the cloister have small single shafts, not the Saracenic coupling to which we have got used in Italy, Sicily, and Southern Gaul. In an odd position to the west of the church, forbidding any west front, is an undercroft with columns with good, but not very rich, twelfth-century capitals, clearly of a piece with the cloister.

Lastly, on the opposite side of the valley, forming a picturesque object on the road from Mortain to the White Abbey, is the small plain church of Neufbourg. The spot marks the solitary dwelling of the Blessed Vital, him who strove to make peace between the contending brothers at Tinchebray, and who gave up his prebend at Mortain and all that he had, to dwell as a hermit amid the woods and rocks.[45] The church, bating a few later insertions, is a perfect Transitional cross church, with a flat east end and no aisles. In this part of Normandy the small churches that one lights on in the villages, though commonly of pleasing outline, have seldom any remarkable work. In this they are distinguished in a marked way from the wonderful series of parish churches round Caen and Bayeux. Those we are tempted to compare with the churches of our own Holland, Marshland, and Northern Northamptonshire. But the comparison does not strictly apply. In each case there is a series of notable churches which never were collegiate or monastic. But in the English district the churches are, as parish churches, of considerable size, sometimes indeed very large, though never affecting the character of a minster. The churches in the Bessin are mainly small, but of singular excellence of work, largely Romanesque of the twelfth century. We may come to some of them before we have done.

MORTAIN TO ARGENTAN

1892

ONE great object in the parts of Mortain is to see the historic site of Tinchebray, so closely connected with Mortain in its history, though the two places are, and seem always to have been, in different divisions, ecclesiastical and civil. We debate whether Tinchebray can be best got at from Mortain, Vire, or Flers. Mortain would be the best way by railway, if only trains ran on every part of the line. But between Sourdeval and Tinchebray no trains now run. We rule then that Tinchebray will be best got at by road from Flers, and owing to the gap on the railway, the way by train from Mortain to Flers is by Vire. We thus get a few hours at Vire. It is the Feast of the Assumption; the great church is crowded with worshippers. It is therefore impossible to make a study of its interior. But we can see that it has a grand nave, nearly of the same style as Mortain, but loftier. There are many additions and changes in the later styles, and the only tower is at the side and of no great height. We would fain see more of this church on some less venerated day. Then there is the gateway with the tower-belfry; there is the donjon on its mound, crowning another of the peninsular heights on which castles rose, this time a real peninsula, with the river below from which the town takes its name. There is a glimpse to be taken of the famous valley of Vire, and we go back to the station to betake us to Flers. It is not altogether for the sake of its own merits that we go to Flers, but because we have ruled that it is on the whole the best place from whence to make the journey to Tinchebray. Flers, we imagine, is as old as other places; but there seems to be nothing to say about it. It has no church of any importance, it has a respectable castle of late mediæval lines, standing in a real moat. This has become in an odd way a dependency of a later house, which happily has not swallowed it up. Flers itself has of late years risen to some importance as a manufacturing town. And we are bound to say that these French manufacturing towns look much cleaner and tidier than their fellows in England. But for historical and antiquarian purposes Flers counts for very little. And it is, after all, possible that it may not be the best starting point for Tinchebray. We cannot say till we have made the attempt from Vire.

We had meant to go by carriage from Flers to Tinchebray, and to take on the way La Lande-Patry the house of that William Patry who appears in Wace as having entertained Earl Harold as a guest at the time of his stay in Normandy. And we did get to La Lande-Patry another day. Strange to say, while De

71

Caumont spoke of traces of the castle in the past tense, Joanne, so much later, spoke of them in the present. At any rate, the thing was worth trying; one might at least muse on the spot. We found the place a little way from Flers, a church and a few houses, called distinctively La Lande-patry, as distinguished from a neighbouring village called by some such name as *La Fontaine de Patry*. The church is not quite wholly new, though it is mostly so; but there is nothing that could have been built or looked on by any one who received Harold. Nor do we distinctly see anything in the way of mounds or ditches. And yet we flatter ourselves that we have lighted on the site. He who has read Wace's story of Duke William's ride from Valognes and of his greeting by Hubert of Rye will remember how Hubert was standing "entre le moutier et la motte."[46] The "moutier" and the "motte," the church and the castle, have, in these places, a way of standing near together. So, having got the church and marked that it stands on a bit of high ground with a slope to the south-east, we run down a lane and into a field to the north-west, and there find a charming site for the "motte." The little hill rises with a fair amount of steepness above a flat piece of land with a small stream wriggling about in it. Then we go on and find that there is a near slope to the north-east also, so we have our "moutier" and the almost certain site of our "motte." They are fixed, as they should be, on one end of a peninsular hill, though we must confess that the hill is not very lofty. Here then, we feel fairly satisfied, it was that William Patry—written, it seems, in Latin *Patricius*—welcomed as a peaceful guest the Earl whom in after-days he was to meet in arms as King on the day of the great battle.[47]

But Tinchebray is much more than La Lande-Patry, and the site is much more certain. There it was, as Englishmen at the time deemed, that the assize of God's judgment on Senlac was reversed after forty years.[48] England had been won by the Duke of the Normans; Normandy was now to be won by a King of the English. To be sure the English King was the son of the Norman Duke; but he was born in England; he spoke the English tongue; Englishmen had chosen him to be their king rather than his purely Norman brother. King Henry's host was most likely far more largely Norman—specially West-Norman—than English; the chief men above all were Norman; still there were Englishmen in it, and those Englishmen looked on the fight as a national struggle and on the result as a national victory. William of Malmesbury witnesses to the feeling; it is odd that there is not a word of it in "Ordericus Angligena," writing at Saint-Evroul. We read our Orderic; we read the little that there is in Wace; we read the contemporary account in a letter by a Norman partisan of Henry. We then go forth to make out what we can of the site, knowing perfectly well that we shall not find a castle standing up as at Falaise.

The railway takes us from Flers to Montsecret junction, and from Montsecret junction to Tinchebray station. We are looking out for a possible site for the battle, and we soon rule that the ground where the station itself stands, the flat ground to the north of the town, will do perfectly well for the purpose; but we do not as yet know whether there may not be some other site which may do equally well. We walk up from the station, and we find Tinchebray itself a somewhat larger town than we had looked for, though still but small. It strikes us almost at once that it is a town of the same class as Carlisle, Stirling, and Edinburgh, where a single long street, with more or less of slope, leads up to a castle at one end. Here at Tinchebray it is the east end, where the castle hill rises boldly enough over the little stream of the Noireau, the Norman Blackwater, which gives a surname to that Condé which became the seat of princes. On the opposite side of the narrow and grassy valley rise higher hills on which King Henry may well have planted his *Malvoisin*. To the south, the hills have withdrawn to a greater distance; the castle hill rises above a meadow which in times past seems to have been a marsh. On the northern side, the hill slopes away more gradually to the plain. Here the castle must have trusted wholly to its own defences. It is on this north side only, where the railway runs, that the battle could have been fought. For the fight of Tinchebray really was a battle, one of the very few pitched battles of the age. The campaign indeed began in an attack on the fortress; but it grew into something more on both sides. And it is only to the north that there was room for the operations of two armies of any size; the earlier besieging could take place from all points, but specially, one would think, from the east and north. But we have to make out these things as well as we can from the look of the ground. The contemporary accounts give us the facts; but they give them without local colouring.

Of the buildings of the castle fairly full accounts have been preserved, which may be studied in a History of Tinchebray in three volumes by the Abbé L.V. Dumaine (Paris: 1883). It is a book most praiseworthy for bringing together all manner of local facts of all manner of dates. And it is full of plans and plates to illustrate particular subjects. For historical criticism we do not look; but we should have liked a clear plan of the castle and town, and, if possible, the reproduction of some old drawing of the castle, such as one often finds. As things are, we have to put up with M. Dumaine's description. Towards the river and the marsh the castle trusted mainly to its natural defences; but at least on the side towards the town it had a ditch which has now vanished. The gates are gone, but the likeness survives of a building near the eastern gate with two pointed arches rising from a pillar, known as *Les Porches*. Here was the *Champ Belle-Noe*, and on the hill on the opposite site of the valley was *Beaulieu*. The names were not ill deserved; the stream and its accompaniments make a pleasant look-out. But of the buildings of the castle nothing now is left; the utmost that we can do is to make out, not the eastern gate itself, but its site. No walls and bulwarks stand up; we must be content with calling up an imagination what there once was. But that is enough; the castle of Henry's day standing up would be best of all; a simple empty space would be next best; but the scattered buildings of the little suburb which occupies the castle site do not seriously hinder us from understanding what we want to understand. In other lines all that Tinchebray has to show is a desecrated fragment of the church of Saint Remigius just outside the castle. Here is a central tower with a very short eastern limb. On the eastern face of the tower is a Romanesque arcade, so very simple and even rude that one is inclined to assign it to a time a good bit earlier than the day of Tinchebray. But there is no such arcade on the other sides, and the western arch of the tower is pointed. What are we to infer when the place is locked and it is hopeless trying to get the key? We do at least remember that the four lantern-arches at Saint David's are not all of the same date; and we hope that, whenever the pointed arch was made, the plain arcade was there on the 28th day of September, 1106, just forty years after the father of the contending princes had landed at Pevensey.

Our accounts are not very clear in their topography, and they do not distinctly point out the site of the battle. The relieving force under Duke Robert and Count William came from Mortain—that is, from the south-west. A striking tale is told of their march. In crossing the forest of *Lande-Pourrie* to the south of Tinchebray the army heard mass under a tree from the mouth of Vital, the holy solitary of Neufbourg. Count William was his lord, if one who had renounced the world could be said to have an earthly lord, and he was only in his allegiance if he accompanied the forces of Mortain. The object of the holy man was to reconcile the brothers, and he made an attempt on the mind of Henry also. But, according to Orderic, the King of the English was able to show that the fault rested wholly with Robert, and that he himself had entered Normandy only from the purest motives. Anyhow arms were to decide. Only on what spot? The south side of the castle, the natural approach from Mortain, gave no opportunities for fighting an open battle, hardly even for an assault on the castle. The ducal army, with William of Mortain and the terrible Robert of Bellême, must have gone round to some other point. The name of *Champ Henriet*, borne by a site to the west of the town, therefore away from the castle, does not seem to prove much. The north side seems to furnish the best fighting-ground, and it is the weakest side of the castle. The King's forces would most likely be on that side, and the Duke would come round to attack them. But one cannot pretend to certainty.

The combatants, some of them, awaken a more lively interest than the immediate scene of their exploits. It is hard to throw ourselves into the feeling of those men of the time who saw in the fight of Tinchebray a national victory of Englishmen over Normans. In some sort it was so; from that day no once could say that a Duke of the Normans held England; it was the King of the English who held Normandy. And the invasion of Normandy by Englishmen and their King, and the fighting of the victorious battle on the forty years' anniversary of the Conqueror's landing, could not have failed to strike men's minds. One strange turning-about of things indeed there was. The man whom Englishmen had once chosen as their King, the heir of Alfred, Cerdic, and Woden, fought at Tinchebray in the following of Duke Robert. Eadgar and Robert had been comrades in the Crusade, and the two men were not unlike in character. Neither could ever act for himself; both could sometimes act for others. And if Eadgar thought at all, he may have seen a rival in Henry, while he assuredly could not have seen one in Robert. Anyhow the Ætheling who had marched on York with Waltheof and Mærleswegen now marched on Tinchebray with William of Mortain and Robert of Bellême. Englishmen may well have seen a truer countryman in the son of the Conqueror, born in England, chosen to his crown by Englishmen and leading Englishmen to battle, than in the grandson of Æthelred, born in Hungary, and fighting alongside of the foreign oppressors whom England and her King had cast out. And the best and the worst of the warrior princes and nobles of the time were there on opposite sides. With Duke Robert came Robert of Bellême, no longer of Shrewsbury or Arundel. With King Henry came the Count of Maine, Helias of La Flèche.

Orderic witnesses to the presence of Englishmen in the battle. The contemporary letter-writer only implies it by mentioning others, of whom he speaks a little scornfully, as well as the men of Bayeux, Avranches, and Coutances, and the Breton and Mansel allies. When Robert of Torigny speaks of the "acies Anglorum," he doubtless simply means, according to a very common form of speech, the force of the King of the English, whatever they might be, either "genere" or "natione." But all who were under the King's immediate command had in some sort to become Englishmen in the hour of battle. Like Brihtnoth and Harold, King Henry stood and waited for the enemy on foot. So did Randolf of Bayeux and the younger William of Warren; so did the wary counsellor who had little love for Englishmen, Robert of Beaumont, Count of Meulan, and presently to be Earl of Leicester, forefather in the female line of another Earl who loved them well. Seven hundred horsemen only kept the two flanks of the infantry. The main body of the horse, Breton and Mansel, stood apart. King Henry's footmen, perhaps with some little advantage of the ground, stood as firm in their ranks as the fathers of some of them had stood forty years before when the lord of Meulan was foremost in the charge against them. They bore up against every charge of the ducal force till Count Helias, with his reserve, chose a happy moment and broke in on their assailants with his horsemen. The lord of Bellême fled for his life; the Duke of the Normans and the Count of Mortain became the prisoners of their conqueror and near kinsman.

The prison of Count William was a strait one. Henry might fairly look on him as a traitor, and it was the general belief that he paid for his treason with his eyes. Here we may perhaps see the groundwork for the foolish story that Duke Robert's fate was equally hard. But Henry was far too wise to commit so useless a crime. The captive Duke spent the remaining twenty-eight years of his life in this castle, and that, treated with all honour, but kept under such restraint as was needful, specially after he had once tried to get away altogether. He did not even cease to be Duke of the Normans. His brother administered his duchy for him; but he never took the ducal title while Robert lived. Robert, in short, was in much the same case as Henry III. was at the hands of Earl Simon. To be carefully looked after at Bristol or Cardiff must have been dull work for one who had scaled the walls of Jerusalem; but in his brother's keeping Robert assuredly never had to lie in bed for want of clothes. As for his comrade Eadgar, he was let go free altogether. The crowned King had no need to fear the momentary King-elect of forty years before. We only wish to know whether he did himself live to so preternatural an age as to be a pensioner of Henry II., or whether he who bears his name in the accounts of that reign is a son of whom history has no tale to tell.

We go back from Tinchebray to Flers. Next day the main line takes us to Argentan. The name of *Tenarcebrai* is written in our own Chronicles; so is that of *Argentses*; only is that really Argentan or only Argences?

———————————

ARGENTAN

1892

A GOOD many of the places which we go through on such a journey as we are now taking in Western Normandy, full as they are of historic and local interest on particular grounds, might easily fail to attract, not only the ordinary tourist, but even the general antiquarian traveller. No one, for instance, need go to La Lande-Patry, unless he is anxious to get a better understanding of a single sentence of the *Roman de Rou*. Even at Tinchebray the strictly historic interest is all. Unless we except that single arcade on the tower of St. Remigius, there is really nothing memorable to show in the shape of either church or castle. With Argentan the case is different. Any one who has a turn for mediæval antiquities in any shape would surely reckon that town as one of high interest. With no such single memory as the great fight of Tinchebray, it plays a certain part in history through many ages; the local history of the town itself is remarkable, and its existing monuments are of various kinds and instructive in several ways. And the means of getting there are as simple as any means well can be; for Argentan is a principal station on the line from Paris to Granville. It is also a station on the great cross line from Caen to Le Mans. This position makes it a good centre for seeing several places in various directions, to say nothing of others for which none of the many railways of Normandy has as yet done anything. In the journey now recorded it served as a centre for Falaise and Séez, and for what will to most people be the less familiar names of Exmes and Almenèches, and it might easily have been made a centre for other places.

Argentan is a kind of town to which it would be hard to find an exact fellow in England. It is not the head of any district; it is not the seat of any great ecclesiastical foundation; such importance as it has in history seems to have come from the presence of a castle which not uncommonly received princely sojourners. Yet it is plainly something more than one of those towns which have simply sprung up at the gate of a castle. It has one main characteristic of a class of towns much greater than its own: the fortress and the great church stand side by side in its most prominent quarter. That in the general view the church is far more conspicuous than the fortress is the result of later havoc; but we are surprised to find that a church of such dignity in itself and placed in such a position as the chief church of Argentan was never the seat of abbot or dean. Falaise is now a larger town than Argentan; but we feel that at Falaise the town has simply grown up at the foot of the castle hill. Saint

Gervase at Falaise is no fellow to the mighty fortress on the *felsen*, as Saint German of Argentan must have been to the *donjon* of Argentan, even when that *donjon* was better seen than it is now. The name of Argentan does not at once lead us to some Gaulish tribe or to some Roman prince; but it does not, like that of Falaise, at once carry its own meaning with it in the speech of some or other of the Teutonic conquerors of Gaul. We feel that Falaise, looking up to the great keep and to the tower of Talbot, is merely a magnificent Dunster or Richmond—we cannot say Windsor; for the *sainte chapelle* of Saint George has no fellow there. But Argentan is a miniature, a very small miniature certainly, but still a miniature, of Durham and Lincoln and Angers. That is, church and fortress stand together on the highest point in the town.

Is Argentan therefore to be set down among the hill-towns? Falaise, of all places in the world, assuredly is not; the castle is set on a hill, but not the town. But can we give the name to Argentan? Some scruple may be felt by one who has come from Saint-Lo, from Coutances, or from Avranches. Yet the ascent from the Orne to the upper part of the town is very marked, and as the chief buildings, ecclesiastical and military, are gathered together on the higher ground, there is a true akropolis. And there is no doubt that this akropolis had its own circuit of wall, distinct from that of the lower town. This last took in a large space, and was of a strangely complicated shape, running out hither and thither in various directions. According to all our experience of other places, we would take for granted that the inner circuit was the older. Here, we should say, was the original settlement; the town, after the usual manner of towns, outstripped its boundaries; it spread itself in whatever directions suited its inhabitants; lastly, the suburbs which thus grew up were taken into the town, and were fenced in by a second wall. This, one need hardly say, is a thing which has happened over and over again, in this place and that, till we take it for granted as the explanation of such a state of things as we see at Argentan. But in a local book, in which a great deal of information about Argentan is brought together, *Le Vieil Argentan*, by M. Eugène Vimont, it is distinctly asserted that the case is the other way. The wider circuit, he tells us, is the older. In the wars of the early days of William, King Henry of France burned Argentan. The burning is undoubted; it is recorded by William of Jumièges. But M. Vimont's inference seems strange—namely, that after this destruction the town was rebuilt, but on a smaller scale. The case would be something like one stage in the history of Périgueux, when only a part of old Vesona was fortified at the time of the barbarian invasion of 407, and the part outside the new walls was forsaken.[49] But an ordinary burning of a town in warfare like that which went on between France and Normandy did not commonly lead to such great changes as this, and it is very hard to believe that the town of Argentan can, in the first half of the eleventh century, have reached this great extent and this irregular shape. We are bound to suppose that a local writer who shows much local knowledge has some reason for what he says. But for a thing so hard to believe some direct authority should be quoted, and M. Vimont quotes none. Till some other convincing authority is produced, we shall believe that the growth of Argentan followed the same law as that of other towns.

It is only in a few small pieces here and there that either the wider or the narrower circuit of wall has left any sign of itself. But we can believe both on M. Vimont's witness, and indeed they hardly need any witness. Each circuit has left its stamp behind it in the way that town walls do leave it, even when, as walls, they have altogether vanished. We hold, then, that the narrower circuit, taking in only the higher ground with the church of Saint German, and the two castles, is the oldest. The church and the *donjon* doubtless had predecessors before King Henry came against Argentan. His burning need not have wrought any more of lasting destruction than a hundred other such burnings. The town sprang up again; in course of time, when Argentan flourished under princely favour, it grew beyond its old bounds. The growth of the inhabited town called for a wider circuit of walls. The new suburbs, with the church of Saint Martin, were taken within the fortified area. Argentan no longer merely looked down on the Orne, but was washed by it.

The upper town, then, besides the church of Saint German, contains not only one, but two castles. On the highest ground of all, in the north-west corner of the enclosure, are the remains of a large polygonal keep, which keeps its name of the *donjon*. It makes very little show, being sadly crowded in by houses. Somewhat lower down is the *château*, a graceful building of the late French Gothic, now used as the Palace of Justice. The building itself has hardly any defensive character about it, but it stands as part of the general line of defence, and it was also connected with the *donjon* by an inner wall, parting the two castles from the town. Some parts of the wall in this neighbourhood, both inner and outer, are still standing; and near the *château* is the desecrated chapel of Saint Nicolas, keeping some good windows.

The *château* would attract anywhere; the fragment of the *donjon* simply peeps over houses. The chief thing in Argentan after all is the great church of Saint German. Both this and the smaller church of Saint Martin down below give us most instructive lessons in the course by which the late Gothic of France gradually changed into *Renaissance*. As we have often said, this transition has in England to be studied almost wholly in houses, while in France we trace it in churches, and grand churches also. The church of Saint German at Argentan is undoubtedly a noble pile. At a distance it suggests the memory of

79

Saint Peter at Coutances on a larger scale. We seem to look on the same grouping of central and western towers, though the central tower of Saint German's is not octagonal, but square. But the western tower at Argentan is not western in the same sense as the western tower at Coutances. That is, it does not stand in the same line with the central tower. It is not a western, but a north-western tower. This allows a greater variety of outline than can be had at Saint Peter's. But the general effect of the towers, all of which evidently received their last finish after the days of pure Gothic had passed away, is essentially the same in the two cases. In the central tower of Saint German this finish is nothing more than a cupola of wood and lead on a handsome but not lofty lantern of late Gothic, wonderfully good, outside at least, for the date of 1555. But the general effect is not bad. The north-western tower, known as *la grosse tour*, has a more curious history. The lowest stage is good and rich Flamboyant, with a highly adorned porch. On this is a much plainer stage, from which the Gothic feeling has passed, but which has no distinctly *Renaissance* detail. It has long narrow windows with flat-arched heads. This must have been building in 1617, when the governor of the town forbade the tower to be carried higher, lest it should overlook the *donjon*. We think of William Rufus bidding Hildebert of Le Mans to pull down his pair of newly built towers.[50] The hindrance was afterwards withdrawn, and in 1638 the tower was finished with its fantastic, but certainly taking, cupola. The nave was begun in 1421, when Normandy was ruled for a season by the descendants of its ancient dukes. It was carried on gradually for 220 years, and was finished in 1641. The changes in style during this time are easily traced. The nave is late but pure Gothic, a really fine design, though a good deal spoiled by the loss of tracery in so many of the windows both in aisles and clerestory. In a large panelled triforium a very keen eye may possibly detect in the lowest range of ornament a tendency—it is nothing more—to *Renaissance* ideas. Or it may only be fancy suggested by the stages further east. Certainly the nave, if not quite of first-rate merit, has a really striking effect, and is far better than most panel work of the time. The transepts are of the same style. They are finished north and south with apses, which are really graceful, though we miss the rose-windows which we should otherwise have looked for in a French church on such a scale as this. The choir too, as seen out of the nave, is well-proportioned and effective, though we see that the windows in the apse have flat arches and no tracery. The apse, if we can call it so, has the strange singularity of ending in a point, and some odd details have crept into the bosses of the vault. But, in the general view from the nave, the only thing that mars the general harmony and good effect is the treatment of the lantern. The four lantern arches have the flattened shape of the latest Gothic; but, oddly enough, the variety here chosen is the English four-centred arch, not the usual French shape, three-centred, elliptic, or actually flat-headed. But both the English and the French form are quite unsuited for pier-arches, and for lantern arches yet more. And, though the work of the lantern is quite good outside, yet within we see that the enemy has begun to take possession. There is perhaps no actual un-Gothic detail, but the feeling of the arcade of flat-headed arches which forms the gallery shows the way in which things are tending.

We go into the choir. There, setting aside the apse windows, the arcade, triforium, clerestory, are still pure, if very late Gothic; the new fashion comes in one detail only; the vaulting shafts have an odd kind of Ionic capital. It is in the latest part of all, the chapels round the choir, that the new taste comes in most strongly, and even there it is not altogether dominant. It is very strange outside, where heavy flying-buttresses are tricked out with little columns. Within, pairs of such little columns are the chief ornament. But they support no arches, only scraps of entablature. The arches of the roof, the windows, and everything else, are still of the elliptic shape, and they still keep the late Gothic mouldings. No building better shows what a long fight was waged between the two styles. Saint German at Argentan is not like Saint Eustace, where we see a grand Gothic conception carried out without a single correct Gothic detail. Here not only the conception, but the great mass of the internal detail, is purely Gothic; the new fashion thrusts itself in only in particular parts.

This last remark is specially true of the smaller church of Argentan, that of Saint Martin. Here we have not the full cruciform shape. There is no central tower or lantern, but only lower transepts projecting from a continuous nave and choir, whose roof-line, within and without, runs uninterruptedly from east to west. The only tower is a small octagonal one with a spire at the north-west corner. The peculiarity within is that, while the arcade and clerestory are still late Gothic, the triforium between them has run off into *Renaissance*. The reason seems clear. The new fashion affected details long before it touched the great lines of the building. The triforium at this date is, as at Saint German, simply a matter of detail, an arrangement of panelling and the like. That stage, therefore, was naturally touched by the intruding foes, while the main features, like the pillars and pier-arches, are as yet not all affected. At Saint Martin the windows are some of them good Flamboyant, while some are a kind of very bad Perpendicular. From others, as at Saint German, the tracery has been cut away altogether. This church, smaller than Saint German, of a less effective outline, and standing in the lower part of the town, has nothing like the same grand effect as the two towers of Saint German on the hill. But it has, with its tall clerestory, a stately look from some approaches, and it has its lesson to tell in the history of art.

One is surprised to hear that in the old days Argentan had but a single *curé*, whose sphere of usefulness took in both Saint German and Saint Martin. One fully expects to find that such a church as Saint German was collegiate. But this is one of the characteristic features of French architecture. We are used in England to great town churches, which never were more than parish churches, covering a good deal more ground than Saint German's. But we are not used, save at Shoreham and Bristol, to see them built, like Saint German, so thoroughly on the type of churches of higher rank. Boston, Newark, Saint Michael's at Coventry, Trinity Church at Hull, are as grand in their way as Saint German at Argentan, only it is in quite another way.

There are a few other things to see at Argentan. On the slope of the hill is a good late Gothic house, with two arches of street arcade in front. Add a little more, and we should have the arcade of Carentan; add a great deal more, and we should have the arcades of Bern. Those who seek for it will also find a mediæval bridge of two pointed arches over one of the branches of the Orne. And it is grievous when, after moving from Argentan to new quarters at Laigle, we take another look at M. Vimont's book, and find that we have failed to see a small desecrated Romanesque church called *Notre-Dame de la Place*. We relieve ourselves by finding fault with M. Vimont, who certainly does not always put things in those parts of his book where we should most naturally look for them.

But we have one point to settle with witnesses nearer home. In the war between William Rufus and Duke Robert, the Duke, with his ally King Philip of France, took a castle in which Roger the Poitevin, son of Earl Roger of Shrewsbury and brother of Robert of Bellême, commanded for William at the head of 700 knights. Strange to say, they all surrendered without shedding of blood on the first day of the siege. Our chronicle calls the place *Argentses*, which Florence of Worcester translates by *Argentinum castrum*.[51] The name looks like Argences, much nearer to Caen than Argentan. But one doubts whether Argences could ever have been a fortress of such importance, perhaps whether it was a fortress at all. And Robert of Torigny, who must have known the country better than anybody at Peterborough or Worcester, has *Argentomum*, which certainly means Argentan, and which may perhaps have the force of a correction. If so, we have a second visit to Argentan by a French king of the eleventh century, but not one which made any new building needful.

There is a good deal more to say about Argentan in later times, from Henry the Second of Normandy and England to Henry the Fourth of Navarre and France. The traveller is most likely to sojourn at the *Hôtel des Trois Maries*, a resting-place which, in its foundation rather than in its buildings, goes back to the fourteenth century. It has received many memorable guests, and its host is said to have purveyed for the last Henry that we have spoken of. It stands in the main street on the lower ground. The thought did suggest itself that it might be a trifle too near the Orne, whose waters at Argentan are not attractively clean, and that the *Hôtel du Donjon* on the top of the hill might have a better air. But we can say nothing as to the further merits or demerits of the Donjon, and the Three Maries sheltered us well enough by the space of six days.

———————————

EXMES AND ALMENÈCHES

1892

EXMES and Almenèches; one fancies that those names will sound strange to almost any one save those who have been lately reading the eleventh book of Orderic the Englishman. Exmes indeed is one of those unlucky places which, even in the year 1891, remain without the comfort of a railway. But Almenèches has a station happily placed on two lines; it is visited by trains between Granville and Paris, and also by trains between Caen and Le Mans. It thus seems to stand in a closer relation to the world of modern times than Exmes, to which he who does not care to trust himself to a Norman omnibus must go on his own account. To Almenèches too one may go on one's own account; each place makes a pleasant drive from Argentan. There is nothing very striking on the road to either, but the road to Almenèches decidedly goes through the prettier country. Each has a church and a castle to show, or rather each has a church and the site of a castle. As in so many places, the ecclesiastical building has outlived the fortress. And this is more to be noticed at Almenèches, where the church was monastic, and therefore ran greater chances of destruction in the days of havoc. In general history we cannot venture to say that either spot has a place. In special Norman history Exmes, under some or other of the forms of its name, *Oximum*, *Hiesmes*, anything else, often shows itself; its early importance is noticed by its giving its name to the large district, *Pagus Oximensis*, *Oixmeiz*, *Hiesmsis*. And the *Oximenses* are sometimes spoken of in a special way, as if they were a distinct people, capable of acting for themselves. Of Almenèches we hardly hear anything but at one particular moment, and then we hear of Exmes along with it.

In short, the history of Almenèches, as far as we are concerned with it, might be summed up under a sensational heading, as "The Sorrows of Abbess Emma." Her sorrows did not last long, but they were heavy while they lasted. It was hard for the head of a devout Sisterhood to have three of the great ones of the earth set upon her at once, one of them being her own brother. She was daughter of Roger of Montgomery, afterwards Earl of two shires in England, and of his first wife, Mabel of Bellême, who bears so evil a reputation for bloodshed and treachery. She was therefore sister to the heir of her mother's estates and crimes, to that Robert of Bellême who is charged with a crime from which the worst Merwing would have shrunk, that of pulling out the eyes of his little godson, seemingly only for the fun of the thing. But Emma and her sisters are described as being much better than any of their brothers, even those who were not so bad as Robert. She may therefore not have been wholly unfit for the post in which she was set when her father put her at the head of his newly founded abbey, though she could hardly have been qualified according to the rule which Gregory the Great laid down for the monasteries of Sicily, that no abbess should be under sixty years of age.

The troubles of Abbess Emma began in the year 1102, when her brother Robert was happily driven out of England, with his brothers and his whole followings and belongings. It might seem a little hard when King Henry, in getting rid of the whole stock, seized on the English lands which Earl Roger had given to his daughter's Norman Abbey. But we remember that, in so doing, he was forestalling, not the Eighth of his name, but the Fifth. We did not want alien priories in England. Robert came back to his native Normandy, began to work every kind of mischief there, and his brothers Arnulf and Roger helped him for awhile in so doing. Arnulf is famous at Pembroke.[52] Roger the *Poitevin*, so called from his marriage, had been lord of that land between Mersey and Ribble, which afterwards went to patch up the modern shire of Lancaster. Presently the brothers quarrelled. Robert of Bellême refused to give Arnulf and Roger any share in their father's inheritance. Then they forsook him, and Arnulf took an active part against him on behalf of Duke Robert. We read how, in June, 1103, he seized his brother's *munitio* of Almenèches, and how it was occupied for the Duke. This was dangerous to his sister's abbey, where his followers did not scruple to occupy the buildings and to stable their horses in the church. Then Robert of Bellême, looking on the abbey as a hostile fortress, comes down on Almenèches, burns the church and all the buildings of the monastery, and leaves his sister and her nuns to find shelter where they can. The Duke's followers, who fall into his hands, he deals with after his manner; they are killed, mutilated, or kept in hard bonds. Robert of Bellême, it must be remembered, is the man of whom it was said that he refused ransom for his prisoners, despising gain, compared with the keener pleasure of tormenting them. The Duke then and his following set forth to do something against the hateful tyrant—"*odibilis tyrannus*" he is called, a phrase in which we must not forget the ancient sense of "*tyrannus*."[53] Counts and lords are with him, and the whole force of the land of Exmes. They hold their councils in the castle of Exmes; they did what they could against the tyrant; but he was too strong for them. He defeated the Duke in battle, and got possession of the castle of Exmes.

Meanwhile Abbess Emma and her Sisterhood had to go whither they could. "Tener virginum conventus misere dispersus est." Some sought shelter with kinsfolk and friends. The Abbess herself and three nuns went to Saint-Evroul, where Orderic, who tells the story, dwelled as the monk Vital. They found a shelter and a place of worship in an ancient chapel where Saint Evroul himself had dwelled—"coelesti theoriae intentus solitarie degebat." There they abode six months, till in the next year they were able to go back to Almenèches and to begin to set up their ruined home again. For ten years Abbess Emma laboured at gathering the sisterhood together and rebuilding the church. Then she died, and, by as near an approach to hereditary succession as could be in the case of abbesses, her staff passed to her niece Matilda, daughter of her brother Philip. She, too, had to rebuild church and monastery after another fire. We are not told how it was kindled: but by that time her uncle Robert was safe in prison in England, shorn of all power of burning anything or of gouging out anybody's eyes.[54]

Our present business is to see the sites of all these events. We hardly dared to hope that we may see any ecclesiastical work of Abbess Emma or Abbess Matilda. Still less do we hope to see the castles which Arnulf and Robert of Bellême seized on standing up as they were in their day. Both Exmes and Almenèches, in the present state of their military works, are among the places which most fully bear out the doctrine with which we started in speaking of Hauteville, that a site is often better when there is nothing on it. The site of the castle of Exmes is not exactly in an ideal state. The best case of all would be if it still bore a castle of the right date; the second best would be if there were only a green hill and its ditch, with full power of walking freely over them as one thought good. The castle-hill of Exmes is not in so happy a case as either of these; but it is much better off than if it were surmounted by a barrack or a prison. The hill is there; the ditch, as we suppose we must call it, is there; there is no building on the hill save a small modern chapel; the only bad thing about it is that the top of the hill is cut up into small fields with high hedges, and that the ditch is cut up into gardens. There is therefore no means either of going freely about, or of taking any connected view of the top of the hill. Still, the general line of the place can be easily made out, and we soon see that a site well suited for its purpose has been made the most of. The actual hill of the castle makes no special show in the distance. No longer marked by the castle itself, it seems simply part of the general mass of high ground on which both town and castle stand, and from which the castle-hill itself stands forward in a peninsular fashion towards the north. The hill is round, or nearly so; and no small measure of human skill has been employed in adapting it to purposes of defence. We spoke of a ditch; but a ditch is hardly the right word. At a good height above the actual bottom, as one feels very strongly in going up the road from Argentan, the castle-hill strictly so called is surrounded by the artificial work which, for want of a better name, we have called a ditch. But it is safer to say that the hill-side has been cut, leaving the upper part of the hill with scarped sides rising above a flat piece of ground all round, which puts on the character of a ditch or not according as the hill-side at different points supplies a bank on the other side. It is on the side towards the town that it is most truly a ditch. The general effect is something like the clerestory of a round church, the Temple Church or any other, rising above a flat-roofed surrounding aisle. The ditch is wide, and doubtless has been deeper—that is, more of a ditch—than it is now; that is, its use for gardens must have raised its general level. One's thoughts somehow rather go away to Marsala than to Arques or Old Sarum—perhaps because in those last we can freely go about, while gardens, houses, what not, come in the way both at Marsala and at Exmes. If they were away, the whole thing would be more like some of the ditches on the Malvern hills than anything else.

Such is all that is to be seen of the castle of Exmes; but, in the absence of an actual donjon that can have seen the wars of the Conqueror and his sons, it is quite enough. The look-out is a wide one indeed; but it is now easier to get it from the road going back to Argentan than from the top of the hill itself. The eye ranges over a vast space chiefly to the north-west, over the great forest of Gouffers, over plains and undulating ground, a wide and striking view, but in which no remarkable object rises up to catch the eye. We look forth with the special hope of getting a distant glimpse of Falaise and its donjon. Perhaps not the donjon itself, but the high ground about it is said to be seen from the tower of Saint German at Argentan. But we at least could not see it from Exmes.

The other object in the little town of Exmes, now hardly more than a village, is the church. This stands on the general mass of high ground from which the castle hill juts out. It is a building of no small interest, both from what it has to show and from what it has not. At first sight it seems utterly shapeless. What first catches the eye is a very pretty apse of good Flamboyant work, with windows in two ranges, of which all in the upper and some in the lower are blocked. We see also at the same glance that something just to the west of the apse has been destroyed or left unfinished. Beyond this again is a much lower western body, a nave with its aisles thrown under one roof. This last is not attractive from without, but when we go in, we find that it is the jewel of Exmes. There is a nave of five bays, perhaps once of six, of the very simplest and purest Romanesque, one of the examples which show how that style, better than any other style, can altogether dispense with ornament. There are no columns, no capitals, not a moulding of any kind. Arches of two orders rise from square piers with imposts, and support an equally plain clerestory. For a clerestory there is, genuine and untouched, though so strangely hidden outside by the great sloping roof. This is all; but we ask for no more; the design, plain as it is, leaves nothing to ask for. One does not rush at a date; it may be twelfth century; it may be eleventh; but, if so, it is of the second half of the eleventh. Plain as are the imposts, they show that the work is of the confirmed Norman variety of Romanesque; there are no Primitive traces hanging about it, such as we see at Jumièges.

The perfection of the Norman nave seems to have been tampered with in later days by cutting through a low transepted chapel on each side. The arches look as if they had supplanted a sixth arch of the nave. But far greater changes were presently designed. As at Gisors, as at a hundred other places, the Flamboyant architects thought the elder building too plain, and above all things too low. In a great number of cases they rebuilt the choir after their own fashion, but never carried the work on to the nave. Here at Exmes the work in the eastern part was never finished. That seems most likely; but it is possible that the work was finished and has been pulled down. The apse at least was done, and very pretty it is; but a tall transept on each side with a large chapel to the east of each, perhaps built, certainly designed, are not there now. Within, there is no vaulting, and a mean wooden roof has been thrown across at about half the proper length. The nave, too, is covered with a wooden roof, a kind of coved roof with tie-beams. A real barrel-vault would be best of all; but a good flat ceiling, such as was common in Romanesque times, would do very well. It is one of the differences between French and English architecture that the French designers always meant or hoped to have a vault; the wooden roof in a French church is always a mere shift. It was the builders of English parish churches who found out that the wooden roof could be made into an equal substitute for the vault, preferred to it by a deliberate taste.

For one very anxious to work out in detail the curious little bit of history with which the two places are chiefly concerned, it might be better, if he could manage it, to take Exmes and Almenèches in a single round. But it is easier to make them the objects of two separate excursions from Argentan. We set out then from that town with a twofold anxiety on the mind. Shall we find any signs of the abbey of the persecuted Emma? We do not give up all hope till we shall see with our own eyes. Shall we find any signs of the "*munitio*" occupied by her brother Arnulf? Signs we may fairly look for, if not for the thing itself. Our guidebook describes a church of Almenèches, but it does not distinctly say whether it is the church of the abbey or a separate parish church. It speaks of a "beau tumulus" in the "environs" of Almenèches, and says that the neighbourhood is full of "equestrian memories," whatever those may be. One of them, to be sure, bears the name of the "Manoir de la Motte," which has a very tempting sound. On the ordnance map we can find nothing of this manor; but we do find "Almenèches" and "le Château d'Almenèches" marked as two distinct *communes*. This is encouraging; we seem to have lighted on what at home we should call "Abbess Almenèches" and "Castle

Almenèches." We see Emma at the one and Arnulf at the other; but we still do not know what traces either sister or brother may have left. At last we reach Almenèches, Abbess Almenèches, and we see the church described in our Joanne. It is not very tempting in its general look, and there is nothing particular about its site, except that the ground does slope away from its east-end. Is this Emma's minster or its successor, or is it merely a parish church, and have we to look for the abbey elsewhere? Some signs of the cloister roof on the south side soon settle this question. But we begin to hope, for the credit of the house of Montgomery, that Emma, either before or after her troubles, and her niece after her, had a better church than this to preside over. We find from Joanne that Almenèches boasts of its church; but it doth falsely boast. Instead of the nave of Romsey or of Matilda's church at Caen, we have a single body of late Gothic, with windows like very bad Perpendicular, a form not uncommon hereabouts. We get its date from an inscription:—

"Ce temple lequel a esté ruiné par l'antiquité fut commencé à reedifier l'a^n de grace 1534 et fut perfaict l'a^n 1550 par revere^{n}de dame Madame Loyse de Silly abbesse de cea^{n}s. Gloire et hon^r. soyt au seigneur."

Louise of Silly's work may be just endured; it is at any rate better than the choir built by a later Abbess Louise—we have got out of the age of Emmas and Matildas—in 1674. That is the lowest depth of all; it is the depth reached by the choir of Saint Wulfram of Abbeville; that is, it is of no style at all; a decent Italian building would be welcome by the side of it. But its modern adornments may teach us the history of Saint Opportuna down to our own day. That may be said, because it represents her translation in the days of the second Republic in 1849. What most strikes one is the appearance in stained glass of modern uniforms and—we were going to say modern bonnets, only we are told that the bonnets of 1849 are not counted as modern in 1891. Still we are sure that neither Abbess Emma nor even Abbess Louise ever wore such before they entered religion. Altogether one never saw so poor an abbey church anywhere. One is curious to know what it immediately supplanted, and whether the sisterhood was again in such straits as those which it had been in the time of Emma of Montgomery. Did the house never recover from the seizure of its lands by King Henry?

Of the "Manoir de la Motte" nothing can be heard. But the "*munitio*" must be represented, at least in name, by Le Château d'Almenèches. Our driver protests that there is no *château* there, only a *commune*. So much the better. If there is no *château* there in his sense, that is, no intruding modern house, we are more likely to find the site of the real *château*, the *munitio*. And we presently do find it. We are going on in some difficulties, amidst a good deal of rain; but we see something in a field by the roadside, between Almenèches and the church of Le Château d'Almenèches which is evidently the right thing. There is a manifest mound and ditch of some kind. We go on to the church, one about as worthless as may be, but which will serve as a place at least of shelter. But by that time the rain has stopped, and we are able to study our mound and ditch without let or hindrance. Here is the castle, the *munitio*, of Almenèches, whence the Duke's followers first troubled Abbess Emma. But yet more, here is Joanne's "*beau tumulus*" thrown in along with it. A plan is almost needed to set forth what we see. Here is a piece of slightly elevated ground girded by a ditch on all sides except where the sluggish river Don— how many Dons are there in Europe?—which in times past clearly supplied the ditch with water, itself flows. Here then is the castle; at least here are its essential features. And they are all clearer, because there is no *château* in the driver's sense, but only a farmhouse of decent age, which does no harm. But then the ditch, on one side at least, is prolonged to follow one side of a much more striking mound, a long mound which is clearly the "*beau tumulus*." We do not like to be too positive about præ-historic tumps, but this certainly looks very like one. Indeed it need not be præ-historic, it may cover the bones or ashes of some invading Northman, who was cut off too soon to be christened, to learn French, and to become the founder of a Norman house. The tump must be older than the *munitio* proper; but we may be sure that the makers of the *munitio* did not leave it out of their reckonings. It had to be guarded; it could not well be lived on. Here then we have found all that we want at Exmes and Almenèches. We understand the scene of the petty war which drove Abbess Emma to Saint-Evroul. We have found our two castles, all that we cared to find of them. We have found our abbey, or at least a successor on its site. And we have both the tump and the church of Exmes thrown in ἐν παρέρλῳ. It is not at all a bad two days' work that we have done in the immediate land of the *Oximenses*.

LAIGLE AND SAINT-EVROUL

1892

OUR next halting-place is Laigle on the Rille, the Rille that runs out to flow by Brionne and the Bec of Herlouin. We choose it as a halting-place less from any merits of its own than because it is the best centre for some very remarkable places indeed, and because the place itself calls up certain associations. There is, perhaps, more interest attaching to the name of Laigle and to the lords of Laigle than to Laigle itself. Its name supplies us with the crowning instance of the singular incapacity of so many in England to understand that these Norman towns and castles are real places. They give surnames to a crowd of men who figure in the English history of the eleventh and twelfth centuries; but, as we have said before, hardly anybody seems to understand that those surnames are taken from places which are still standing, and to most of which the railway is open. There is the renowned Bishop William of Durham in the days of the Conqueror and the Red King, the greatest name in the history of Romanesque art. He is *Willelmus de Sancto Carilefo*, just like William of Malmesbury or William of Newburgh, simply because he had been monk and prior in the monastery of *Sanctus Carilefus*, in modern form, *Saint-Calais*, in the land of Maine. It is better to say "William of Saint-Calais" than "William of Saint-Carilef," because the use of the modern form shows that we know where the place is; but "William of Saint-Carilef" is not so bad as "Bishop Carilef," as if Carilef were no place at all, and as if it had been usual in those days to talk of Bishops or anybody else by their casual surnames. So with Laigle, *Aquila*, a place which must have somehow taken its name from an eagle, possibly from some incident or legend, as there is certainly nothing in the look of Laigle to suggest eagles in a general way. Its lords of course called themselves "Gilbertus," "Richeras," or anything else "de Aquila," "of Laigle." On the whole, for the same reason as in the case of Saint-Calais, it is better to speak in English of the place and its lords by the now received form *Laigle* rather than *L'Aigle*, though *L'Aigle* is not quite forgotten on the spot. But the events of the Norman Conquest brought men of the house of Laigle into England, and their presence led to a possession in Sussex being called "Honor de Aquila." When South-Saxon antiquaries, or possibly lawyers, of whatever age, translated this into "the Honour of the Eagle," they plainly did not know that *Aquila*, *Laigle*, was a real place from which men had taken their name and brought it into Sussex. And we have heard of an Englishman being christened "Richard de Aquila," as if it were hopeless trying to put "de Aquila" into plain English. We have also heard of a man being christened "Joseph of Arimathæa"; but that was at least in English, and not in French, Latin, or Hebrew.

"Richard de Aquila" is a form notable on another ground, as implying a confusion between the two wholly distinct names of *Richard* and *Richer*. We do not at this moment remember a Richard of Laigle, but Richer of Laigle is, perhaps, the man of his house who is best worth remembering. He lived in the days of the Conqueror, he bears the best character possible in those times, and his one recorded act bears it out. He was fighting for William, Duke and king, against that castle of Sainte-Susanne in Maine which the Conqueror of Le Mans and Exeter could not take. In a skirmish below the castle a beardless-boy, sheltered behind a thicket, aimed an arrow which gave Richer a mortal wound. His comrades would have killed the lad; but Richer bade them spare him; his own sins deserved death. For want of a priest, he confessed those sins to his comrades, and died.

The lords of Laigle did plenty of other things besides this; but it is the thought of the last act of Richer which cleaves most firmly in the memory, and makes us most wish to see the place where the lords of Laigle dwelled. And we set out with some vague notion, a notion not exactly to be fulfilled, that the home of the lords of Laigle—"domini de Aquila"—must be something of an eagle's nest. But alas, when we reach Laigle from Argentan, we find that, with all its historic associations, it is in itself far from being a town of the same interest as Argentan. The position of the two is quite different. The chief buildings of Argentan cover a small hill in the midst of scenery in no way strongly marked. Laigle covers the slope of the hill which forms one side of the valley of the young Rille, while another height matches it on the opposite side. At Laigle the chief church, standing out with a dignity which it hardly keeps when we come near to it, is the one striking object. Of the castle we see nothing but the surrounding woods, and in truth there is nothing more to see. The large brick house known as *le vieux château*, standing a little to the east of the church, marks, it is to be supposed, the site of the home of Richer and all the rest of the brood of the eagle. But no site of any castle can well be further from the eagle's nest which we came in search of. The town, as distinguished from castle and church, has little or nothing to show; like Flers, it has risen to some modern importance through manufactures. The chief church, St Martin, has already struck us on our approach by its stately tower of late Gothic such as in England we might have looked to see crowned with battlement and pinnacles, but which here is finished with a high roof bearing statues on its ridge. Beside the tower there is something, one hardly knows what, a very high roof and a kind of spire. When we come near, we find that the church, though very short, has two western towers. The northern one is the rich piece of Flamboyant work with which we have already got familiar—

or rather not familiar, as its narrow windows may in the distance be taken for a Romanesque arcade. Its southern fellow is a real Romanesque tower with pilaster buttresses, which bears the spire. It is very plain, of the eleventh century rather than of the twelfth, so that the lord of Laigle, who awakens an interest above the rest of his house, may have looked at it or even built it. The same may be said of the apse which ends the central of the three bodies—they are hardly to be called nave and aisles—which make up the church of Laigle. But a Romanesque apse, rich or plain, is not improved by first cutting pointed windows in it and then blocking them up. And the apse, thus sadly mutilated, is further imprisoned. It barely peeps out between the east ends of the northern and southern bodies, of which the northern takes the form of a kind of transept. They are in the worst style of the late French Gothic, with windows of the same wretched Perpendicular as those of Almenèches. Whence came this strange taste? Henry the Fifth and John Duke of Bedford might, somewhat earlier, have taught their Norman subjects to build good Perpendicular, but not this kind of stuff.

There is not much more to see in Laigle itself. Of the castle we can hardly be said to have even seen the site. The house which represents it has ceased to be a *château* even in the latter sense. It stands pleasantly at the end of the town, with fields beyond it, and a good slope down to the river, if only it could be seen. But the whole way from the castle to the Rille is blocked with modern buildings. We wish that the home of Richer was in the same case as the head of the *Oximenses*, where the gardens in the ditch do comparatively little harm. Or rather we cherish a hope that the *vieux château* may not be the true *castrum de Aquila*. We cannot say that we saw any other castle anywhere else at Laigle; but we saw one or two sites higher up the hill where a castle might have stood very fittingly.

But the main object at Laigle is not Laigle. The place may be used, like Argentan, as a centre for seeing several objects, and in the case of Laigle the objects to be seen from the centre are certainly of higher interest than the centre itself. There are the famous border castles of Verneuil and Tillières, easily to be reached by railway, and there is an ecclesiastical spot of still higher fame which can in a rather complicated way be reached by railway, but which it is pleasanter and certainly more appropriate to take by road. Yet as a means of approaching Ouche, Aticum, Saint-Evroul, even the road seems too modern. It is essentially a place of pilgrimage, not a Canterbury pilgrimage, but a pilgrimage to the cell of a hermit, to the *scriptorium* of a chronicler of whom we get more personally fond than of any other.

At Saint-Evroul we ought to think first of all of Saint Evroul; we do think first of all of Orderic the Englishman, called in religion Vital.[55] We called him just now a chronicler; but that is assuredly not his right description. If he were more of a chronicler, that is, if he told his story in a more orderly way, without so many repetitions and runnings to and fro, that is, if he were other than the kindly, gossiping, rambling old monk who has made Saint-Evroul a household word for all students of English and Norman history in his own day we ought not to feel so warmly drawn to him as we are. It was the home of Orderic that we wished to see. But it was very hard to find out whether his home had anything left to show us. Not a word could we find in any guidebook to say whether the abbey was living or ruined or desecrated or wholly swept away. It might be as unlucky as Avranches or as lucky as Saint Peter-on-Dives. And a monastic site from which everything monastic has been swept away is not so instructive as a fortified site from which the fortifications are gone. We should be best pleased to find at Saint-Evroul a church in which Orderic may have worshipped, but it would be better to find a later church—we had almost said one with discontinuous imposts to its pillars—rather than no church at all. We set forth in faith, not knowing what we are to find, but determined that we will at least see the place where the Ecclesiastical History of Normandy was written. One little incident of the journey may be mentioned. We reached Saint-Evroul; we saw more of Saint-Evroul's Abbey than we had ventured to hope that we should find there. But before we reached it our driver stopped near a house and buildings which seemed in no way attractive. Asked why he stopped there, he said that was where the landlady at Laigle had told him to stop. There were the great glass-works for which Saint-Evroul is now best known. And it was the Saint-Evroul of the glass-work that we were thought to have set forth to see, not the Saint-Evroul of Orderic or of Saint Evroul himself.

Orderic, son of a French father and an English mother, born by the banks of the Severn ten years after King William came into England, in the year of the martyrdom of Waltheof, was before all things Orderic the Englishman. If we are to take his words literally, English must have been the only language of his childhood. He was sent in his childhood to be a monk of Saint-Evroul;[56] one wonders why, as his father might surely have found him a cell either in the Orleans of his birth or the Shrewsbury of his adoption. Himself more truly the founder of Shrewsbury Abbey than his patron, Earl Roger, Odelerius of Ettingsham, the married priest, preferred Saint-Evroul to any other house of religion as the home of his son. The Abbey had lately been set up again, after a time of decay, by the bounty of several members of the houses of Geroy and Grantmesnil, one of whom, Abbot Robert, who plays also a part in Calabria and Sicily, was at least as turbulent as bountiful. But nothing would have more deeply grieved the monastic soul of Orderic than the thought that any one could think more of him than of the local saint and first founder. "Father

Evroul," "Pater Ebrulfus," the man of the world who turned hermit in the days of Chlotocher, and around whose cell the monastery first grew up, lived in the devout memory of his spiritual children. One asks whether Orderic, "tenellus exsul" in his Norman monastery, like Joseph in Egypt hearing a strange language, ever stopped to think of the true meaning of his patron's name, how the softened *Ebrulfus* and *Evroul* disguised the two fierce beasts which went to make up the name of *Eoforwulf*. Perhaps, indeed, Orderic the Englishman, and all other Englishmen, had some right to see a kinsman, however distant, in the saint who bore so terrible a name. For Ebrulfus came of the city or land of Bayeux, and in Chlotocher's day, and long after, the land of Bayeux was still the *Otlingua Saxonica*, an abiding trace of those harryings and settlements of Sidonius's times, which planted the Saxon on both sides of the Channel. Still, to us Orderic is more than Evroul, even in the form of Eoforwulf. It is for his sake that we take our journey through the wood of Ouche till we come to the little stream of the Charenton, where the hermit chose out his solitary cell, where the monastery twice arose in his honour, and where now the glass-works are thought to be a greater attraction than the monastery.

The remains of the abbey soon catch our eye, as we draw near from the east side, the side of Laigle. They are not placed quite at the bottom of the valley; they gently climb up the hill to the west, the hill up which the small low street of Saint-Evroul leads to the highest point, where we find another sign of our own day in the railway station. The church of the monastery is a mere ruin; but it at least stands open to the sky; it is not desecrated and disfigured by being put to any profane use. Quite enough is left to put together the whole plan of the building. There is perhaps a slight feeling of disappointment at finding that here at Saint-Evroul there is nothing directly to remind us of the man for whose sake we have come thither. We would fain see something that had met the eyes of the island-born child in the first years of his coming to his foreign home. We would fain see even the church of Robert of Grantmesnil, much more the elder church from which the High Chancellor of Duke Hugh the Great carried away the body of Saint Evroul himself, as a piece of holy spoil which Normandy had to yield to France.[57] We would fain see the cloister where in Orderic's day, King Henry of England, victor of Tinchebray, sat a long time in thought, and the chapter-house where the Lion of Justice conferred with the brethren, where he praised their good order and devotion, and was, at his earnest request, admitted to their spiritual fellowship. And truly nowhere in kingdom or duchy had he a more loyal subject than the chronicler who knew so well what a work it was to bring some approach to peace and order into a land torn in pieces by noble brigands. Hopes of this kind, hopes of any immediate memory of the days of Orderic or of days before Orderic are not fated to be gratified; but we have done well to come to Saint-Evroul none the less.

The ruined church offers us much to see and study. The only thing that suggests itself as a possible memorial of Orderic's day is the foundation of the apse. But as it is only a foundation and not a crypt, there is no need to think that he ever saw it. The apse itself has fallen; but traces enough are left to show that inside at least it was polygonal. But it was an apse of the old simple pattern, without surrounding aisles and chapels. It could not have been there when the young novice from Shropshire came to Saint-Evroul. It may have been built in the latter part of his long sojourn. And the stumps of the great round pillars of the choir are most likely of the same date. The use of such pillars is a fashion English rather than Norman; but it is hard to believe that the "tenellus exsul" from Ettingsham brought with him any architectural tastes. The choir was of some length, and its length was broken by an apsidal chapel on each side, pointing north and south, so as to form a kind of small eastern transept. But the greater part of what is left is very fine work of the thirteenth century, finished at the west end in the fourteenth. The pillars and arches of the nave are broken down, leaving only stumps; but enough is left at the west end and at the crossing to show the design. Clustering shafts surrounded a central pillar; the mouldings of the arches are, as often happens in Normandy, as well and deeply cut as they would be in England. Above the arcade was a tall clerestory, seemingly without any triforium or with the triforium thrown into the clerestory. Altogether there is about enough left to suggest the memory of Glastonbury, though Saint-Evroul is certainly not on the scale of Glastonbury, even without the western church. The west front must have been very remarkable. The first impression on approaching from outside is that two western towers stood out in front of the nave, as at Holyrood, or as the single towers at Dunkeld and Brechin. A second glance shows that what seemed to be the lower part of a south-western tower is really a building in advance of such a tower. That is to say, a large porch, or rather portico, with three tall arches, stood out in front of the western towers and of the end of the nave. It must have looked just enough like Peterborough to suggest Peterborough, but also to suggest the contrast between Peterborough and itself. At Peterborough the great portico stands indeed, as here, in advance of a west front with two towers. But it may be said to have supplanted that front. One tower was never finished; the other was thrown into insignificance. The portico is of the full height, and became the real west front. Here at Saint-Evroul the portico was not the whole of the west front, but only part; the towers must have risen a long way above it. One would like to be able to judge of the effect of such a design.

There is little or nothing left of the other buildings of the abbey, except the gateway by which we enter, with a larger and a smaller pointed arch. The field to the south of the church, where cloister, chapter-house, refectory, and the rest must have stood, had a locked gateway, and the owner had gone off with the key. But there seemed to be nothing, at least nothing standing up. Yet we should have liked to see at least the traces of the cloister on the southern wall. But Saint Evroul is not forgotten in his own place, or even within the walls of his own abbey. For a little chapel has been made within the buildings of the gate-house. He has also a cross and fountain, of which the cross, a modern one, is more visible than the fountain. And in the parish church on the opposite hill some relics of the abbey, indeed of the saint himself, are still preserved. There is specially a good fragment of an ancient triptych. The surviving small church looks down on the relics of the great one below. And the thought comes, so different from any suggested by the monastic ruins of England, how short a time it after all is since the great church of Saint-Evroul was a living thing as well as the small one. A visitor of no wonderful age could do a sum and find that his own father was at least able to walk and talk while Robert of Grantmesnil had still a less famous, but perhaps less unquiet successor.

———————————

TILLIÈRES AND VERNEUIL

1892

OUR second excursion from Laigle has quite another kind of interest from that of Saint-Evroul. We go more strictly to see places, and not as it were to commune with a single man. And the places that we go to see are primarily military, and not ecclesiastical. We do not go for a great church, not knowing whether we shall find it perfect or ruined, or wholly swept away. We go to see two castles or sites of castles, knowing that we shall find something more than their sites, and with a notion that we shall also get something ecclesiastical thrown into the balance. Our object is to see the two border castles of Tillières and Verneuil, both easily reached by railway from our central point at Laigle, and which by a more roundabout way, may be reached from Evreux also. Tillières is famous in the early wars of Normandy and France. Verneuil is best known in the days when Normandy had become the battle ground of England and France, and when Scotland threw herself on the French side. As a matter of fact, we saw Verneuil first; we then went on to Tillières, and thence back to Laigle, getting of course a second clear view of Verneuil by the way. But it will be more convenient to speak first of the place of more ancient fame.

Tillières, Tillières on the Arve, if it were left in its ancient state, would be an almost ideal border-fortress. It is close indeed on the border. When Wace describes Alençon, he tells us that one side of the water was Norman and the other side was Mansel. So here at Tillières one side of the water was Norman and the other side was French. But the stream of Arve at Tillières is so much narrower than the stream of Sarthe at Alençon that French and Norman stood much nearer together at Tillières than Mansel and Norman stood at Alençon. Alençon again, as far as its history goes back, has always been a considerable town. Tillières is now a mere village, except so far as so many of these villages put on the character of very small towns. But town or village, Tillières is simply something which has grown up at the foot of the castle, while at Alençon one might say that one object at least of the castle was to defend the town. There is high ground on each side of the stream; that on the north side is Norman soil, that on the south is French. A projecting point of the Norman height was seized for the building of the great border-fortress of Normandy. A few dwellings of men, dependants doubtless of the castle and its lords, arose under its shadow, just within the Norman border. That this was done while France and Normandy were still foreign and hostile lands is shown by the western doorway of the church of Tillières, a piece of plain Romanesque, of late eleventh or early twelfth century. Meanwhile, it does not appear that the opposite height was crowned by any French fortress. Tillières must have been a standing menace to France, without there being any standing menace to Normandy back again. Here are our topographical facts, very clear and simple, quite enough to account for the part which Tillières plays in the history of the Norman duchy.

That part may be told in a few sentences, but it is a striking story none the less. Tillières, *Tegulense castrum*, bears a name cognate with the Kerameikos of Athens and with the Tuilleries of Paris. It was first fortified by Duke Richard the Good, the Duke who would have none but gentlemen about him, and in whose days the peasants arose against their masters. He gave his sister Matilda in marriage to Odo, Count of Chartres; he gave her lands by the Arve as her dowry; but when she died childless, he held that he had a right to take them back again. To this doctrine the widower naturally did not agree; disputes arose between the two princes, and the fortress of Tillières—one would like to know its exact shape in those days—arose as a bulwark of Normandy, beneath whose walls the Count of Chartres underwent a defeat at the hands of Duke Richard's lieutenants. They were Neal of Coutances and Ralph of Toesny, speaking names in Norman history. We next hear of Tillières in the young days of William the Great, when King Henry could no longer endure such a standing menace to France as the castle above the Arve. It is the Norman writers who tell us, and we have no French tale to set against this, how the King of the French demanded the castle of Tillières—how the young duke's guardians found it prudent to yield to his demand—how its valiant governor, Gilbert Crispin, refused to give it up—how the united forces of France and Normandy constrained him—how the border-fortress was burned before all men, while the King swore that it should not be set again for four years. But they go on to tell us how the faithless King went on into the land of Exmes, how he burned Argentan, and came back to fortify Tillières again as a bulwark of France against Normandy.[58] Time passed on. King Henry fought with Duke William at Val-ès-dunes, and fled before him at Varaville; and, as a fruit of the last Norman victory, Tillières passed back again to its old use as the border defence of Normandy.

With such a history as this, and with a site so well suited to the history, one could wish that there was more at Tillières to describe than there actually is. We should be best pleased of all if the castle hill of Tillières was still crowned with an ancient donjon; next to that we should like to see it in the same case as Exmes or rather as Almenèches. But the height is taken possession of by a house of much more pretension than the harmless farm at Almenèches, and the passing wayfarer can do little more than follow the outer wall of the castle

—a wall with work of endless dates—round a good part of its compass. Looking down from the height, looking up from the village, best of all perhaps from a point of the railway just west of the Tillières station, the general relations of castle, village, stream, and the once hostile hills beyond, can be well taken in; but not much more than the general relations. And the village has little to show beyond its church; and there the Romanesque doorway is the choicest thing, as being part of our chain of evidence. But it seems not to be on this ground that the church of Tillières is counted among "historic monuments," that is, forbidden to be pulled about by any one else, but destined sooner or later, to be pulled about by the national powers. Its qualification for admission into this class seems to be the *Renaissance* choir. On the outside this is about as poor a jumble of bad Gothic and bad Italian as can well be thought of; within it has a somewhat better effect with a vault and rich pendants. Still they are nothing like so striking as those in Saint Gervase at Falaise, which do really make us wonder how they are kept up. More really interesting, perhaps, is the wooden roof of the nave, evidently as great a feat as a French artist was capable of in the way of wooden roofs. And an eye from Somerset looks kindly at this outlandish attempt to make a kind of coved roof, and to paint it withal. Such a one hopes that the French Republic will not turn diocesan architect, and try to get rid of it. But he thinks that he could show better coved roofs at home, and he wonders why, if the coved shaped was chosen, a system of South-Saxon tie-beams and king-posts was thrust in as well.

We turn to the other famous border-fortress of Verneuil. Here the position, as a position, is in no way to be compared to that of Tillières; but we have one grand military tower; we have a much larger town, containing several important churches and houses, and one ecclesiastical tower which may claim a place in the very first rank of its own class. Verneuil is a border-fortress; but it is not so ideal a border-fortress as Tillières. It is not so close on the border; for here Normandy has a small *Peraia*, a certain amount of territory beyond the river. And, as Verneuil presented no such commanding point for a castle site as Tillières did, the fortress was not placed on a height at all, but in the lower part of the town, to guard the stream. There is a distinct ascent in Verneuil; but nothing like the slope at Tillières from the Norman castle down to the border-stream and from the border-stream up again to the French hills. But there is enough rise to make the grand ecclesiastical tower on the high ground stand out as the most prominent object in the approach, while the grand military tower down below makes no show at all. We were a little puzzled by Joanne's account of Verneuil, in which he said that the castle had been completely demolished, but that the donjon existed still. It seems that at Verneuil, as at Argentan, castle and donjon are distinguished; but at Verneuil castle and donjon are not, as at Argentan, separate buildings joined only by a long wall; they stand close together and formed part of one work. Nor is the castle as distinguished from the donjon, completely demolished; there is a considerable fragment standing very near. The donjon, called locally *Tourgrise* from the colour of its stone, is a round tower, not quite a rival of Coucy, but tall enough and big enough to have a very striking effect. It has been lately restored or set up again in some way, perhaps cleared out and roofed in. Anyhow Verneuil is not a little proud of the fact, and marks its thankfulness by a great number of rather foolish inscriptions. The tower is proclaimed to be the work of Henry I., our Henry of Tinchebray, not the developed rebuilder of Tillières; but this seems out of the question, as the small doorways—we cannot guarantee the windows—have pointed arches, which seem to be original. But the ruined fragment of the castle hard by, with its ruder masonry and a shattered round-headed window seemed certainly to be as early as Henry's day and very likely a good bit earlier. Hard by the donjon seems to be a small piece of town walls; otherwise the walls have vanished, and are, as usual, marked by boulevards. That on the north side still keeps the character of a rampart, and is a good place for studying the most visible ornaments of the town.

Verneuil has much to show both in churches and houses. Of the latter, besides a good many of timber and brick, which are always pleasant to see, there are two which are more remarkable. One is a singularly good bit of late Gothic with windows and a graceful *tourelle*. The other has a *tourelle* of the same kind, but it runs off into *Renaissance*. Both have a curious kind of masonry, squares alternately of brick and stone. The greatest church is that of Saint Mary Magdalen, in the great open place in the upper part of the town. Here is the grand tower, built between 1506 and 1530, a noble design, and carried out without any infection of foreign detail. It is practically detached, standing at the south-west corner of a low nave. If the nave had ever been rebuilt, as was doubtless designed, to match the later and loftier choir, the effect of the tower would have suffered a good deal. As it is, from some points, where the nave is not seen at all, it reminded one a little of Limoges Cathedral, as it stood before the rebuilding of the nave was begun. It rises by two tall stages above the church; then the square tower changes to an octagon, a very small octagon supporting one still smaller. It would have been far better to have given the octagon more importance, as in most of the other great examples, French and English, starting with Boston stump. It is further complained, and the complaint is true, that the upper part of the square tower looks top-heavy. It was just the same with the other Magdalen tower at Taunton till its rebuilding. Since then, strange to say, though no difference of detail can be seen in the rebuilt tower, the effect of top-heaviness is gone. In both cases that effect was, doubtless, due to the piling of stage upon stage, without making them gradually increase in lightness and richness towards the top, as at Bishops Lydeard. But it is not a case to find fault; the vast height, the grandeur of design, the purity of detail at so late a time, all mark this tower as one of the noblest works of the late French Gothic. A little way to the west is another tower, attached to a now desecrated church, we believe of Saint John, which was clearly built as a rival to the Magdalen tower. It is rather smaller, and in its lower stages plainer—no fault in that; but a little higher it begins to Italianise, and then stops altogether. An ugly modern top is all that answers to the upper stages and octagon of the Magdalen. The people of the Magdalen parish must have been strongly tempted to say of their nearest neighbours, "These men began to build, and were not able to finish."

The church to which this most stately tower is attached is not of any great interest, beyond a simple Romanesque doorway and window in the west front, and some very plain arches to match in the transepts. The choir is rather poor late Gothic, spoiled by a great blank space between arcade and clerestory. Of the nave we hardly know what to say. As it stands, it is plainly modern; the great round pillars are hollow; but the design is one which we can hardly fancy coming into anybody's head, unless it reproduced something older. It is something like Boxgrove, something like some German churches, but not exactly. A pair of pier-arches are grouped under a single arch containing a single clerestory window, and there is a barrel-vault above all. A church in the hands of Huguenots, called "La Salle des Conférences," seems to have a Romanesque shell and keeps three windows in a flat east end. Not far from the donjon is the Decorated church of Saint Lawrence, where the usual late Gothic dies off into *Renaissance* at the west end. But the other great piece of ecclesiastical work in Verneuil, besides the Magdalen tower, is the choir of the church of Our Lady, lower down in the town. There is an east end, such as one hardly sees on so small a scale out of Auvergne. Here is the apse, the surrounding aisle, the apses again projecting from the aisle; and the varied outline is made yet more varied by a round turret of the same date and style thrown in among the apses. The general air is early, the work plain, the masonry simple; but the clerestory windows have pointed arches. We gaze with delight on an outline more thoroughly picturesque than we have seen for a long while, and which carries back our thoughts to a land of which all the memories are pleasing. We purpose to look at it once more before we finally turn away from Verneuil; but good intentions are not always carried out. Let us dream of another Arvernian journey, so planned as to take Verneuil on the road.

BEAUMONT-LE-ROGER

1892

THE name of Roger of Beaumont must be well known to any who have studied the details of the Norman Conquest of England, though Roger's own position with regard to that event is a negative one. His sons play a part in the Conquest itself, and yet more in the events that followed the Conquest. In the reign of Henry I. Robert of Meulan, son of Roger of Beaumont, but called from the French fief of his mother, is the most prominent person after the King himself and Anselm. But Roger himself, the old Roger, stayed in Normandy as the counsellor of Duchess Matilda, while his eldest son followed Duke William to the war. There is interest enough about the man himself and his belongings to give attraction to the place which specially bears his name, and which, in truth, was his own creation. The man and the place are called after one another. Roger is the Roger of Beaumont; Beaumont is the Beaumont of Roger. He was not always Roger of Beaumont; he first appears as Roger, son of Humfrey *de Vetulis*. One learns one's map of Normandy by degrees. The description of *De Vetulis* is a little puzzling; it has been turned into French and English in more ways than are right. But get out at the Beaumont station of the Paris and Cherbourg Railway—it comes between Evreux and Bernay—and walk to the little town of Beaumont, and a fresh light is gained. Perhaps it strikes us for the first time, perhaps it comes up again as a scrap of knowledge lighted up afresh, when, between the station and the town, we pass through the *faubourg* of *Les Vieilles*. How it came by the name we need not ask; the name was there and is there, and we see that Humfrey *de Vetulis* is simply Humfrey of *Les Vieilles*. We see that here down below was the earliest seat of the house, till Roger climbed the *Bellus Mons*, to found his castle, to give it his name, and to take his name from it. It is a pleasant process when these small facts come out on the spot with a life that they can never get out of books. A scoffer might ask whether it were worth while to go to Beaumont-le-Roger simply to get a clearer notion of the meaning of the words "Humfredus de Vetulis." But it is clearly worth while to go to Beaumont-le-Roger, both for the association of the place and to see what Roger made and what others have made since his day. At Hauteville we could simply guess at the spot which may have witnessed the earliest wiles of Robert the *Wiscard*: there is no doubt at all as to the scene of the earliest wiles of one who might have been called Robert the Wiscard just as truly. Here were spent the early days of Robert, son of Roger, great in three lands—Lord of Beaumont, Count of Meulan, and Earl of Leicester, forefather in the female line of the most glorious holder of his earldom.[59]

We walk from the station with the *Bellus Mons* plainly before us in a general way, in the shape of a well-wooded range of high ground. But we see no castle standing up. An abiding castle of Roger's day we hardly look for; but we do not even see any special mount rising above the pass of the hill, or standing out as a promontory in front of it. The most prominent object is the parish church nestling at the foot of the hill. We see that it has a rich tower; we presently see that it has also one of those wonderfully lofty choirs, which seldom get westward as far as the tower, but which, if they did, would cut down the tower to insignificance. We are used to these things; we know that the work that we see must be late; but that does not cut off the hope that the church may contain something of the age of Roger or his sons. A building of Roger's youth would be something precious. It would rank with Duchess Judith's Abbey at Bernay, with the long and massive nave of the church at Breteuil, in which, notwithstanding modern tamperings, we are tempted to see a work of William Fitz-Osbern, while he was still only lord of Breteuil, and not yet Earl of Hereford. But of Roger and his house the church of Beaumont has no signs; all is late, save the pillars with Transitional capitals, which peep out. The choir is very late, and in its details very bad; here, as in a hundred other places, we wonder how men who had such grand general conceptions could be so unlucky in the way of carrying them out. The aisles have some good Flamboyant windows, and the tower, if it had been carried up to its full height, would have been a fine example of the style. And against it now lean two memorial stones commemorating founders and foundations, but not of the house of *De Vetulis*. They are brought from the neighbouring abbey, of which we shall presently have to speak.

Close above the church we take a road up the hill-side. It is well to turn presently, to take in the strange grouping of the tower and the tall choir, as seen from a point a little above them. But our object now is that which is historically the central, physically the loftiest, point at Beaumont, the castle on the *Bellus Mons* itself. We soon begin to see fragments of masonry rising above us on the left hand. Here, then, is the castle; and so in a sense it is. That is, it is part of its works, within its precincts; but it is not the head work of all. We go on a little further, and we see signs of mound and ditch plainly enough. But we do not take in their full grandeur, till we are kindly admitted within the gate of one of the small holdings into which the site of the fortress of Roger's rearing is now cut up. Then we see, indeed, why it was that "Rogerius de Vetulis" was changed into "Rogerius de Bello Monte."

It is, indeed, a "*bellus mons*" in the sense of commanding a wide and pleasant outlook. The town and church of Beaumont, from some points the abbey close below, the wide vale of the Rille and the hills beyond, make up a cheerful landscape. But if by the *"bellus mons"* we were to understand a fair natural hill, we should be led astray. The actual site of Roger's keep is neither a natural hill nor an artificial mound. It is a piece of the natural hill artificially cut off from the general mass. The founder chose a point of the hill-side which suited his objects. Its southern face, towards the open country, was steep enough for purposes of defence; for the rest, he cut off the piece of ground that was to be fortified by a gigantic ditch in the form of a horse-shoe. It is a ditch indeed, one that gladdens the eye that is looking out for such things. There is not so much of it, but what there is seems as grand as anything at Arques or Old Sarum. Lilybæum stands apart; Roger must have had plenty of labour at his command; but he had not, like the engineers of Carthage, to dig through the solid rock. It is a ditch to look down on from above, and also to walk along in its depth, and to look up on each side. The ground is not absolutely open all round; some obstructions of farm-buildings, and the like, hinder one from stepping out the horse-shoe quite as far as it goes; but the top of the mound—if mound is the right word—is perfectly free. There are fragments of masonry left everywhere, *but* there is no continuous wall anywhere, nor any scrap of detail by which we could fix a date. Still, enough is left for all purposes of historical association, enough to show in what kind of a place Roger of *Les Vieilles* fixed his home. It is not exactly an eagle's nest; for that kind of dwelling Normandy supplies fewer opportunities than some other lands. But it comes much more nearly to an eagle's nest than the home of any lord of Laigle who dwelled at Laigle. The exact ground-plan Mr. Clark, and few besides Mr. Clark, could make out. But without making out the exact ground-plan, we learn enough to teach us not a little about both Roger's Beaumont and Beaumont's Roger.

Was the lord of Beaumont-le-Roger entitled to a *sainte chapelle* in his castle? Perhaps he might seem to be so when he was also Count of Meulan and Earl of Leicester. Perhaps it might seem so still more when Beaumont had come into the hands of French kings, and had begun to be granted out as a *comté-pairie* for their sons. But, seemingly before that time, which did not come till the fourteenth century, a building arose which is not exactly a *sainte chapelle* within the castle, but which is very near to the castle, and which has very much the air of a *sainte chapelle*. When we speak of a *sainte chapelle* we, of course, mean a *sainte chapelle* anywhere, whether at Riom, Paris, or anywhere else. This building is the abbey church of Beaumont, which stands just below the castle on the hill-side, a building once evidently of remarkable beauty. Perhaps the most notable feature about it is the ascent from the road below to the abbey buildings, a covered passage lighted by large early Geometrical windows. We make our way up and presently reach the abbey itself. It is plain that on this narrow ledge on the hill-side it was no more possible than it was on the steep of Saint Michael's Mount to put the several buildings of the monastery in their accustomed relation to the church and to one another. Too much has perished for any one but a specialist in monastic arrangements to attempt to spell out the buildings of the monastery in detail; but it seems that a good deal lay to the westward of the church which in ordinary cases would have been placed to the north or south. The church is but a fragment; the north and east walls are there, and from them we can reconstruct it. "East Wall" is here a phrase that may be used; for we are a little amazed to find that the church had no apse, but an English-looking flat end. The large east window has lost its tracery, which should have been something of the pattern of the Angels' Choir at Lincoln. The whole of the work that remains is of the best French Early Gothic. Seen from below, from the bridge across the Rille at no great distance, there is something wonderfully striking in this single side of the church, an inside seen from outside, with its sheltered windows and vaulting-shafts, standing against the side of the castle-hill. How was it when both abbey and castle were perfect? As it is, the abbey is the more prominent of the two. We can see at least a piece of it, while we have to guess at the castle; none of its fragments stand out at any distance. Yet, even looking thus, the abbey seems something subordinate, something dependent; it seems crowded into an unnatural position in order to be an appendage to something else. The parish church stands out boldly enough. It has a right to do so; it came in the order of nature. It proclaims the separate being of the town of Beaumont. The town of Beaumont doubtless sprang up because of the presence of the castle; but it sprang up by an independent growth; it was not the personal creation of any of its lords. The abbey, on the other hand, placed on so strange a site, was clearly the personal device of its own founder, who may have felt a number of very different feelings gratified, as he saw an abbey of his own making at his feet.

The result is an abbatial church unlike all other abbatial churches. The abbey of Beaumont is very beautiful, while the abbey of Almenèches is very ugly; yet Almenèches comes one degree nearer than Beaumont to one's ordinary notion of an abbey church. The abbey of Beaumont must have been a lovely chapel, but only a chapel. If it stood in its perfect state at Caen, among that wonderful group of noble minsters and great parish churches, it would strike us as a beautiful, but a small thing. This is not the usual position of the church of an abbey. It was, in fact, a pious and artistic fancy; while not, in strictness of description, a *sainte chapelle* or other chapel of a castle, it has all the effect of being such. Or in its position against the hill-side, it may call up the memory of Brantôme far away in Périgord;[60] it has nothing in common with a typical abbey church like Saint-Evroul, except the accident of being much of the same date and style.

One building still remains to be noticed in the Beaumont of Roger. That is the church of his earliest home at Les Vieilles. It had, or was meant to have, a pretty thirteenth-century tower. But the church is a mere fragment, mutilated, desecrated, shut up. A decently kept ruin is far less offensive than a church in such a state as this. But the thought again comes, as at Saint-Evroul, how short a time has passed since the parish church of Les Vieilles and the abbey church of Beaumont were both living things. No man now alive can remember them such; but not so many years back many could. In 1861 we talked with one who remembered the abbey church of Bernay in the full extent of its choir and Lady-chapel. We go back after thirty years to find the church of the Conqueror's grandmother in other things much as it was, still desecrated, but with no more of actual destruction. But we find that the one genuine Roman shaft that was there, one of the very few such north of Loire, has either perished or has been so covered up with timber framework as to be quite out of sight. And one later, but still early capital, had been knocked away to make a convenient resting-place for a wooden beam. One would think that such a building as this, even if it cannot be restored to divine worship, might at least be made *monument historique* and taken care of. Only then the State would some day come and take away every real shaft and every real capital, and put imitation shafts and capitals in their stead. And that might be even worse than the wooden beams.

JUBLAINS

1876

WE know not how far the name of Silchester may be known among Frenchmen, but we suspect that the name of Jublains is very little known among Englishmen. The two places certainly very nearly answer to one another in the two countries. Both alike are buried Roman towns whose sites had been forsaken, or occupied only by small villages; both have supplied modern inquirers with endless stores both of walls and foundations and of movable relics; and the two spots further agree in this, that both at Silchester and at Jublains the history of the place has to be made out from the place itself; all that we can do is to make out the Roman names; we have no record of the history of either.[61] The names which the two places now bear respectively illustrate the rules of French and English nomenclature. Silchester proclaims itself by its English name to have been a Roman *castrum*, but it keeps no trace of its Roman name of Calleva. But Næodunum of the Diablintes follows the same rule as Lutetia of the Parisii. The old name of the town itself is forgotten, but the name of the tribe still lives. The case is not quite so clear as that of Paris; some unlucky etymologists have seen in the name Jublains traces of *Jules* and of *bains*; but a moment's thought will show that the name is a natural corruption of *Diablintes*. The name is spelled several ways, of which *Jublains* is now the one in vogue; but another form, *Jublent*, better brings out its origin. As for the two places themselves, Jublains and Silchester, each of them has its points in which it surpasses the other. At Silchester there is the town-wall, nearly perfect throughout the whole of its circuit. Jublains fails here; but, on the other hand, Silchester has no one object to set against the magnificent remains of the fortress or citadel, the traditional camp of Cæsar. Silchester again has the great advantage of being systematically and skilfully dug out, while Jublains has been examined only piecemeal. This again illustrates the difference between the state of ownership in England and in France. Silchester is at the command of a single will, which happily is in the present generation wisely guided. Jublains must fare as may seem good to a multitude of separate wills, of which it is too much to expect that all will at any time be wisely guided. But it is worth while to remember on the other hand that a single foolish Duke may easily do more mischief than several wise Dukes can do good, and that out of the many owners of Jublains, if we cannot expect all at any time to be wise, there is a fair chance that at no moment will every one of them be foolish.

At the present moment most certainly several of the owners of Jublains are the opposite of foolish, and the most important monument of all is placed beyond the individual caprice of any man. The great fortress is diligently taken care of under the authority of the local Archæological Society; the theatre is the property of M. Henri Barbe, a zealous resident antiquary and the historian of the place; and the other chief remains are easily accessible, and, as far as we can see, stand in no danger. But it is of course impossible to dig up the whole place in the same way as Silchester has been dug up. The modern Diablintes must live somewhere; no power short of that of an Eastern despot can expel them all from the sites of their predecessors, even to make the ways and works of those predecessors more clearly known.

But we have as yet hardly said what and where Jublains is. It lies in the old county and diocese of Maine, in the modern department of Mayenne, on the road between the towns of Mayenne and Evron. The site was, as the local historian well points out, one admirably chosen for the site of a town, standing as it does at the point of junction of the roads from various parts of Central and Northern Gaul and from the Constantine and Armorican peninsulas. It stands on a gently sloping height, with a wide view over the flatter land to the south, and over the Cenomannian hills more to the east, the peak of Montaigu, namesake of our own Montacute, forming a prominent object. The traveller coming along the road from Mayenne, the most likely point of approach, will hardly notice anything remarkable till he reaches the parish church, a building of no special importance, but which has a bell-gable of a type more familiar in Britain than in Gaul. Here, if he has any eyes at all, he will see that the church is built on the foundations of some much larger and earlier building. The masses of Roman masonry are clear enough, with two round projections near the two western angles of the church. These are the remains of the *thermæ* of Næodunum, and the traveller has in fact passed through the greater part of the ancient city to reach them. There are plenty of other and far greater remains; but this is the only one which lies immediately on the road by which the traveller is likely to come. The enclosed space of the town was an irregular four-sided figure, with no distinct four streets of a *chester*, but rather with a greater number of ways meeting together, like our Godmanchester. The whole eastern side of the town is full of remains among the fields and gardens; not far from the northern entrance, a field or two away from the road, are the very distinct foundations of a temple locally known as that of Fortune. A walk over two or three more fields, crossed by traces of foundations at almost every step, brings the traveller to a more singular object, known locally as *La Tonnelle*, which looks very much like the foundation of a round temple, such as that of Hercules (late Vesta) at Rome. And something like the effect of such a temple is accidentally preserved. A line of trees follows the circular sweep of the foundations, and their trunks really make no bad representatives of the columns of the temple. In short, when the traveller is once put upon the scent, he finds scraps of ancient Næodunum at every step of his walk through Jublains and its fields.

But the most important remains of all lie in the south-western part of the old enclosure. To the extreme south of the city lies the theatre. This is happily the property of M. Barbe, who lives and carries on his researches within its precinct. Its general plan has been made out, and, as diggings go on, the rows of seats are gradually becoming visible. It differs from the shape of most other theatres, as its curved line occupies more than a semicircle, like the shape of a Saracenic horse-shoe arch. It seems that no signs of an amphitheatre had been found at Jublains; so M. Barbe is driven to the conclusion that the same building must have been used for both purposes. How far this is archæologically sound we must leave to those who are specially learned in amphitheatres to determine. But we cannot forget the dissatisfied audience in Horace who, between the acts, or even during the performance itself, called for "aut ursum aut pugiles." The position, sloping away to the south, is indeed a lovely one, and we may congratulate the man who has found at once his home and his work on such a spot.

But the great sight of all at Jublains, that which gives its special character to the place, but which has also a history of its own distinct from the place, has yet to be spoken of. We have kept it for the last, both because of its special history and because it seems to be the only thing which is locally recognised as a place of pilgrimage. Tell your driver to take you to Jublains, and he will at once take you to "le camp de Jules César." He knows the other objects perfectly well; but, unless he is specially asked, he assumes that this one point is the object of the journey. Nor is this wonderful; for the camp, fortress, citadel, whatever it is to be called, though most assuredly not the work of the great Dictator, is after all the great object at Jublains, which gives Jublains its special place among Gaulish and Roman cities. More than this, it is the one object which stands out before all eyes, and which must fix on itself the notice of the most careless passer-by. Suddenly, by the roadside, we come on massive Roman walls, preserved to an unusual proportion of their height. Their circuit may in everyday speech be called a square, though strict mathematical accuracy must pronounce it to be a trapezium. Near the entrance we mark some fragments gathered together, and the eye is regaled, as it so often is in Italy and so seldom in Britain and Northern Gaul, with the sight of the Corinthian acanthus leaf. The wall itself, on the other hand, is of that construction of which we see so much in Britain and in Northern Gaul, but which is unknown in Rome itself. Here are the familiar layers of small stones with the alternate ranges of bricks. We enter where the eastern gate has been, and find a second line of defence, a wall of earth, square, or nearly so, but with its angles rounded off, with its single entrance near the south-east angle carefully kept away from either of the approaches in the outer wall. Within this again is the fortress itself, again quadrangular, with projections at the angles. The more finished parts of its walls, the gateways, and the parts adjoining them, give us specimens of Roman masonry whose vast stones carry us back, be it to the wall of *Roma Quadrata* at one end or to the Black Gate of Trier at the other, and which specially call back the latter in the marks of the metal clamps which have been torn away. Details must be studied on the spot or in the works of M. Barbe, which is nearly the same thing, as they seem to be had only on the spot. But there are not many remains of Roman work more striking than this, and it is more striking still if we try to make out its probable history from the internal evidence, which is all that we have to guide us.

That this fortress does not belong to any early period of the Roman occupation is clear from its construction, the alternate layers of brick and stone, and the bricks with wide joints of masonry between them, as in all the later Roman work. And again, the fact that among the materials of the fortress have been found pieces of other buildings used up again might suggest that it was not built till after some time of change, perhaps of destruction, had come over the city. But it is the numismatic evidence which clearly parts off the history of the fortress from the general history of the city. Jublains has no inscriptions to show, but its numismatic wealth is great. Among the many coins found, not many are earlier than the time of Nero, and those which there are are chiefly coins of Germanicus. From Nero to Constantine coins of all dates are common. It is M. Barbe's inference that it was in Nero's reign that the place began to be of importance, and that its great temple was built. But the numismatic stores of the fortress taken by itself tell quite another story. There, not a coin has been found earlier than Domitian, nor one later than Aurelian, saving a chance find of two Carolingian pieces of Charles the Bald and a modern French piece of Charles the Sixth. Again, though coins are found from Domitian onwards, it is only with Valerian and Gallienus that they become at all common, while the great mass belong to Tetricus and his son. One alone is of Aurelian. That is to say, of 169 coins found in the fortress, 151 come in the twenty years from 258 to 273, while 110 belong to the single reign of the Tetrici. After Aurelian there is nothing earlier than Charles the Bald. It is clear then that the fortress must have been deserted in the reign of Aurelian; it is clear that the time of its chief importance must have been just before, in the time of Tetricus. It looks as if the fortress had had but a very short life. The conclusion of the local antiquaries is that it was most likely raised by Postumus, and that it perished in some revolt or sedition, or merely as the result of the overthrow of Tetricus by Aurelian. A mere glance at the building would have tempted us to put it a little later, to have set it down as part of the defences of Probus, or even of some Emperor much later than Probus. But the numismatic evidence seems irresistible; it seems impossible to escape the conclusion that this splendid piece of Roman military work belongs to the middle of the third century, and that it was forsaken, most likely slighted, within a very few years after its first building.

This is as curious and conclusive a piece of internal evidence as we often light upon; but it must be remembered that all this applies only to the fortress, and not to the town of Næodunum. That had a much longer life. It began long before the fortress, and it went on long after. The diggings at Jublains have brought to light a great number of Christian Frankish objects, which shows that the place kept on some measure of importance long after the Teutonic conquest of Gaul. It seems also to be looked upon as a kind of secondary seat of the Cenomannian bishopric. But it must either have died out bit by bit, or else have perished in some later convulsion. The local inquirers seem to incline to attribute the final destruction of Næodunum, the City of the Diablintes in the nomenclature of the time, to the incursions of the Northmen in the ninth century. That they did a great deal of mischief in Maine is certain; and is a likely enough time for the city to have been finally swept away as a city, and to have left only the insignificant modern village which has grown up amongst its ruins.

Jublains then, Diablintes, Næodunum, whatever it is to be called, has a special place among fallen Roman cities. Aquileia and Salona once ranked among the great cities of the earth; their destruction is matter of recorded history. The destruction of Uriconium is so far matter of recorded history that a reference to it has been detected in the wail of a British poet. The fall of Anderida was sung by our own gleemen and recorded by our own chroniclers. But the fall of Calleva and the fall of Næodunum are alike matters of inference. Geography shows that Calleva fell in the northern march of Cerdic, and the most speaking of all Roman relics, the treasured and hidden eagle, abides as a witness of the day when our fathers overthrew it.[62] Næodunum seems to have undergone no such overthrow as those wrought by the Hun, the Avar, and the Saxon. But the evidence of buildings and of coins reveals to us a most important and singular piece of the internal history of the Roman province of Gaul. The city of the Diablintes itself may have been finally swept away by Hasting or Rolf; but the greatest thing in Næodunum, the Roman fortress, must have been, perhaps broken down, certainly forsaken, by the hands of men who called themselves Romans, while its bricks and stones were still in their first freshness. Nowhere is the truth more strongly brought home to us that there is another kind of evidence besides chronicles, besides even written documents, the evidence of the works of the men themselves who did deeds which no one took the trouble to record with the pen or with the graving tool.

———————————

THE CHURCHES OF CHARTRES AND LE MANS

1868

IT is sometimes curious to see how far the popular fame of buildings is from answering either to their architectural merit or to their historic interest. Take, for instance, the two cathedrals of Chartres and Le Mans, two cities placed within no very great distance of one another, on one of the great French lines of railway, that which leads from Paris to Brest. Chartres is a name which is familiar to every one; its cathedral is counted among the great churches of Christendom; men speak of it in the same breath with Amiens and Ely. Le Mans, on the other hand, is scarcely known; we suspect that many fairly informed persons hardly know where the city itself is; the cathedral is hardly ever spoken of, and, we believe, is scarcely at all known, except to professed architectural students. Yet, except that Chartres is nearer Paris of the two, one is as accessible as the other; the historical associations of Chartres, as far at least as Englishmen are concerned, certainly cannot be compared to those of Le Mans; there is nothing at Chartres to set against the early military and domestic antiquities of Le Mans; the secondary churches of Le Mans distinctly surpass those of Chartres; though between the two cathedral churches the controversy might be more equally waged. Each has great and diverse merits; but for our own part, we have little hesitation in preferring Le Mans even as a work of architecture; that it is a building of higher historic interest there can be no doubt whatever.

Both cities belong to a class of which we have few or none in England. A Celtic hill-fort, crowning a height rising steeply from a river-side, has grown into a Roman city, and the Roman city has remained to our own times the local capital, alike civil and ecclesiastical. It would be hardly possible to find a single town in England whose history has run the same course—a course which is by no means peculiar to Chartres and Le Mans, but which they share with many other cities in all parts of Gaul. And Le Mans especially has a local history of unusual interest, and that history is written with unusual clearness on the site and the earliest remains of the town. But on that history we shall not at present enlarge. Our present object is to compare the churches of the two towns, especially the two great cathedrals, which, as usual, stand within the earliest enclosure, and therefore upon the highest ground in their respective cities.

Two or three events connect the cathedral of Chartres with general and with

English history. The first church of which any part survives is that raised by Fulbert, the famous Bishop of Chartres in the early part of the eleventh century, and the most diligent letter-writer of the time. To this work, of which a vast crypt still remains, our great Cnut was a benefactor. The dignity of the Lord of all Northern Europe has so deeply impressed the writer of Murray's Handbook that he cuts him into two, and speaks of the contributions of the Kings of England, France, and Denmark. In the latter part of the next century, John of Salisbury, so famous in the great struggle between Henry and Thomas, held the Bishopric of Chartres. It was the spires of Chartres to which Edward the Third stretched forth his hands when his heart smote him at the sound of the thunder, and he vowed to refuse no honourable terms of peace. In was in this cathedral that Henry of Navarre received the crown of France, a new holy oil of Marmoutiers being extemporized to supply the place of the inaccessible holy oil of Rheims. The history of the city and county in earlier times is closely mixed up with those of France, Normandy, Anjou, and Champagne. The counts of Chartres and Blois in the tenth, eleventh, and twelfth centuries were men of importance in their day, and one of them directly connected himself with England by a memorable marriage. Chartres was long the dwelling-place of the excellent Adela, the daughter of the Great William, the mother of King Stephen and of the famous Bishop Henry of Winchester. But, while Chartres was thus closely, though indirectly, connected with our history, it never, like Le Mans, actually formed a part of the dominions of a common sovereign with England and Normandy.

The cathedrals of Chartres and Le Mans are about as unlike as any two great mediæval churches well can be. Well nigh the only point of likeness is that each possesses a magnificent east end of the thirteenth century, of the usual French plan, with the apse, the surrounding chapels, the complicated system of flying buttresses. But at Chartres this east end is part of a whole. The crypt still witnesses to the days of Fulbert, the lower stages of the western towers to those of Adela and to those of John of Salisbury; but all the rest of the church, including of course all the interior, is of an uniform style and design. The church throughout follows the usual type of great French churches; the eye accustomed to the buildings of England or Normandy misses the central towers of Lincoln or of Saint Ouen's, but Chartres is not in England or in Normandy, but in France, and its church is built accordingly. A fairer question of taste is raised by the unequal spires of the west front—a French feature again, but occasionally extending into Normandy and England, as at Rouen, Llandaff, Lynn, and Canterbury as it was. But it is only in so long and varied a front as that of Rouen Cathedral that it is at all satisfactory. At Chartres the great south spire is modern and of iron, but we believe it very well reproduces the outline of the elder one of wood, and it certainly comes down heavily and awkwardly upon the towers and upon the roof of the church. The upper part of the north tower is frittered away with work of a later style. Still, allowing for the diversity of the towers, which of course does not appear inside, Chartres is a whole—a consistent, harmonious whole, of great, though we cannot think of first-rate, excellence. How does such a whole stand as compared with a building of strange, and at first sight, unintelligible outline, formed by the juxtaposition of two parts, each of admirable merit in itself, but which startle by their absolute contrast in every way? Chartres was made, Le Mans eminently grew; and different minds will be differently inclined in the comparison between a single harmonious work of art and a union of two buildings widely differing in date, style, and proportion. But, on the other hand, it must be said that nothing at Chartres equals the parts of Le Mans taken separately, and that, in the inside at least, the incongruity of Le Mans is far from being felt in the unpleasant way that might have been looked for.

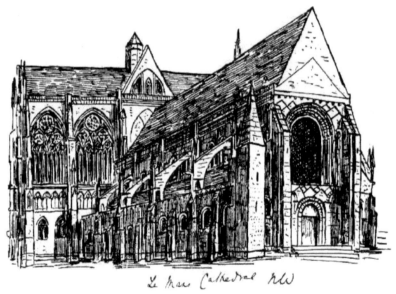

Le Mans Cathedral, N.W.

The general effect of Le Mans Cathedral, as seen from any point but the east, is certainly perplexing. From the east indeed, from the open place below the church and the Roman wall, once a marsh, the apse, with its flying buttresses and surrounding chapels, rises in a grandeur before which Chartres is absolutely dwarfed, and which gives Amiens itself a very formidable rival. We here see the main source of our difficulties, namely that the church has but a single tower, and that at the end of the south transept. Viewed from any other point—looking up, for instance, at the old town from the other side of the river—what one sees is a lofty body with a tower at one end of it, which one is inclined rashly to assume to be the nave, with a western tower, and a lower body joining it at right angles. This last is the real nave of the church, and a magnificent building it is. The truth is that, at Le Mans, as in various other churches in France, the Gothic builders, from the thirteenth century onwards, designed a complete rebuilding. They began at the east, they rebuilt the choir and transepts, but they never got any further, so that the ancient nave remains. So it is at Bordeaux and Toulouse; so it is at Beauvais, where the small but precious fragment of early work, which looks like an excrescence against the gigantic transept—the *Basse Œuvre*, as it is locally called—is really the ancient nave—.[63] So it is in a certain sense at Limoges, where a gap intervenes between the finished choir and transept and the western tower of the original design. But in none of these cases, as far as we can see, can the elder nave have at all approached the grandeur of the noble work at Le Mans. It is a Romanesque building of the eleventh century, reconstructed in the gorgeous style which prevailed towards the end of the twelfth. The outer walls, except in the clerestory, are of the former date, and the contrast in the masonry is very striking. Within, the whole has been recast in the later form of Romanesque, but it has not been wholly rebuilt. Columns with rich and highly classical capitals, supporting arches which are just pointed, have been inserted under the massive round arches of the original church, but the arches are still there and visible. The triforium and clerestory have been wholly reconstructed, or so thoroughly disguised that the old work does not appear. This nave is one of those buildings which, in the infancy of vaulting, their builders found it convenient to vault with one bay of vaulting over two bays of arcade, as in the choir of Boxgrove in the next century. The result is that the piers are alternately columnar and clustered. Setting aside a few of the very grandest buildings of the style—as one would hardly compare this nave with Peterborough, Ely, or Saint Stephen's—this Romanesque nave of Le Mans is one of the finest works of its kind to be found anywhere. And its juxtaposition with the superb Gothic choir is less incongruous than might have been looked for. The only fault is that, as it now stands, the nave ends abruptly to the east with a mere vaulting rib, without any proper choir-arch. But this fault is fully balanced by the glorious view of the choir thus given to the whole church. That any one could compare the inside of Chartres with the inside of Le Mans, thus seen, seems incredible. The height of Le Mans is said to be a few feet greater than that of Chartres. It looks half as high again. At Chartres the height is lost through the great width, and through the use of a low spring for the vaulting arch. At Le Mans everything soars as only a Gothic building, and pre-eminently a French Gothic building, can soar. The pillars, of enormous height, support the clerestory without a triforium. But the effect of the triforium is there still. The aisles are double, and the inner range —itself of the height of the nave of Wells and Exeter—is furnished with a complete triforium and clerestory, which, seen between the pillars of the apses, allow the sort of break which the triforium gives to be combined with the grand effect of the full unbroken columns. Something of the same kind is found at Bourges, and, on a much smaller scale, at Coutances. The effect of the arrangement comes out in perfection at Le Mans. Altogether, little as the building seems to be known, the thirteenth-century work at Le Mans undoubtedly entitles it to rank among the noblest churches of the middle ages. One point more on the Romanesque church of Le Mans. The original design embraced two towers at the end of the transept, like Exeter, Ottery, and seemingly Saint Martin's at Tours. These towers were destroyed by order of William Rufus, who charged the Bishop Hildebert with having used them to shoot at the neighbouring castle.[64] The north tower has never been rebuilt; its ruins are there to this day. The southern tower was again rebuilt at the end of the twelfth century and finished in the fifteenth. This is surely as speaking a bit of architectural history as one often finds.

Interior of Le Mans Cathedral

The writer in Murray, in his zeal for the cathedral of Chartres, assumes that no one will care to visit such inferior buildings as the other churches of that city. Let no man be thus led astray. In the general view of the city from the walks to the south-east, one of the most effective views to be had of any city, two other churches stand out very strikingly, the cathedral crowning all. Of these Saint Anian, we must confess, is somewhat of a deceiver. The distant effect is good, but there is little to repay a nearer examination. It is far otherwise with the Abbey of Saint Peter, whose apse, though on a far smaller scale, is distinctly more skilfully managed than that of the cathedral. The disused collegiate church of Saint Andrew has some good Transitional work, and

Saint Martin-in-the-Vale, just outside the town, is a gem of bold and simple Romanesque. But the secondary churches of Chartres do not equal those of Le Mans, while Chartres is still further behind Le Mans in military and domestic remains. At Le Mans the Abbey of La Couture (*de culturâ Dei*) is a perfect minster with two unfinished western towers, a nave of Aquitanian width,[65] a fine Romanesque apse, in which, if later windows have been inserted, some small fragments of some early work have also been preserved. Beyond the Sarthe is another fine Romanesque church, also a complete minster, the church of Notre-Dame-du-Pré. A fine hospital, the work of Henry the Second, is now perverted to some military purpose, and some military tomfoolery forbids examination, in marked contrast to the liberal spirit which allows free access to everything that the antiquary can wish to visit at Fontevrault and at Saumur. But the ecclesiastical remains of Le Mans are far from being the whole of its attractions. Its military and civil antiquities are endless, and they are more characteristic. We have not the least wish to depreciate Chartres. It is a highly interesting city; it contains a magnificent cathedral and several other remarkable buildings. But it cannot compare with Le Mans.

St. Martin-in-the-Vale, Chartres

Apse of La Couture, Le Mans

_____

LE MANS

1876

WE spoke some years ago of the architectural character of the chief churches of Le Mans, especially in comparison with those of Chartres. But the comparison was of a purely architectural kind, and hardly touched the general history and special position of the Cenomannian city among the cities of Gaul. That position is one which is almost unique. The city of the Cenomanni, the modern Le Mans, has never stood in the first rank of the cities of Europe, or even of Gaul; but there are few which are the centres of deeper or more varied interests. Le Mans has at once a princely, an ecclesiastical, and, above all, a municipal history. It is true that its princely and its ecclesiastical history are spread over many ages, while its municipal history is a thing of a moment; yet it is the municipal history which gives Le Mans its special character. Le Mans, in the course of its long history, has been many things; but it is before all things the city of the *commune*. Among cities north of the Loire—it might perhaps be unsafe to say among cities north of the Alps—Le Mans shares with Exeter the credit of asserting the position of a civic commonwealth in days when, even in more Southern lands, the steps taken in that direction were as yet but very imperfect. And it was against the same enemy that freedom was asserted by the insular and by the continental city. The freedom of Exeter and the freedom of Le Mans were alike asserted against the man who appeared in Maine as no less distinctly the Conqueror than he appeared in England. Exeter, in her character of commonwealth, checked the progress of William by the most determined opposition that he met with in the course of his insular conquest. Le Mans, conquered before William crossed the sea, threw off his yoke when he was master of the island as well as of the mainland. Had the men either of the island or of the mainland been capable of any enlarged political combinations, England and Maine would have done wisely to unite their forces against the common enemy. And it is just possible that those obscure dealings of Earl Harold with the powers of Gaul, which are dimly alluded to by the biographer of Eadward, may have had some object of this kind. But, if so, nothing practical came of them. Maine and England did nothing to help one another. In fact, when Maine was won back to William's obedience, the work was largely done by English hands, and those the hands of men who, there is some reason to think, had Hereward himself as their captain. The actual relations between England and Maine in the eleventh century were thus the exact opposite of what they ought to have been. Englishmen appeared on the mainland as the ravagers and conquerors of a district whose people ought to have been their closest allies. Still even this kind of negative relation does establish a kind of connexion between Maine and England. Above all, it establishes a special analogy between the English city which withstood the Conqueror, and the Gaulish city which revolted against him, in the name of the same principle which a century later was to do such great things among the cities of Lombardy.

The moment then of greatest interest in the history of the Cenomannian city is the moment of its short-lived republican independence. In the case of Le Mans, as in the case of Exeter, we should be well pleased if we knew more of the exact form of commonwealth which it was proposed to establish, and, above all, of the relations which were to be maintained between the city and the surrounding districts. Most likely nothing of the kind was ever put into shape. The commonwealth of Le Mans and the commonwealth of Exeter both sprang into being in a moment of patriotic enthusiasm, when the city and the surrounding districts were fully united in a vigorous effort against the common enemy. How the two were to get on together in more settled times they most likely did not stop to think. What we do know is that the citizens of Le Mans made a *commune*, that the people of the country at large zealously supported them, that the nobles swore to the new commonwealth unwillingly, and, in some cases, even dishonestly. All that we know about the matter comes from the historian of the Cenomannian Bishops, who first of all thinks the *commune* which the Norman Bishop naturally opposed to be a very wicked thing, but who afterwards, when it came to actual fighting, cannot help sympathising with the men of his own city. There was a *commune* of Le Mans, a *commune* in which all Maine shared, a *commune* which the Bishops and the nobles had to join against their will, and which one of the nobles betrayed as soon as he could.[66] That is about all our knowledge; it is just enough to make us wish to know a good deal more. It is enough to throw over Le Mans and Maine an interest which is shared by no other city and province of Northern Gaul; and it makes us feel a kind of disappointment in the inevitable fact that the greatest moment in the history of the city is exactly the one which has left no trace in its existing monuments.

Of the times earlier and later than the republican movement of the eleventh century Le Mans has abundant remains of all kinds. No city is more distinctly the Gaulish hill-fort which has gradually swelled into the Roman, the mediæval, and the modern city. Yet the height of Le Mans is neither so lofty nor so isolated as those of many of its fellows. It is not a detached hill at all, nor does the city stand on the highest ground in its own immediate neighbourhood; and on the eastern, the inland side, the slope of the rising ground is very gradual. Yet the site of the hill-fort which grew into the city was happily chosen. It was pitched on the point where the high ground comes close to the river Sarthe and rises precipitously above it. From the river side then, the western side, Le Mans has most distinctly the character of a hill city, which comes out much less strongly in the approach from the east, while in the approach from the north, where there is an actual descent into the ancient city, it is altogether lost. It is from the river side then that those who wish— while there is yet time—to get a notion of what the Cenomannian city was, either in Roman or in mediæval times, must go to look for it. The city has extended itself on this side as well as on the others, but it has extended itself in the form of an outlying suburb beyond the river. To the west, the north, and the south, the spread of the modern town has done much to wipe out the ancient landmarks.

The Roman remains of Le Mans show well how the conquering race in their distant foundations knew how to adapt themselves to every kind of position. There was one type of city which was preferred wherever the ground allowed of it; but that type was freely forsaken whenever practical necessity commanded that it should be forsaken. The hill of Vindinum, Suindinum, Subdinnum, whichever form we are to choose, therein differing from the hill of Isca, was not at all suited for the laying out of a city according to the familiar type of a Roman *chester*. The high ground immediately overlooking the river formed a long narrow ridge, and the space included within the Roman walls—*la Cité*, as distinguished from the more modern parts of the town—shows no approach to a square, but forms an irregular figure, which only by a stretch of courtesy can be called even an oblong. Within this again the chief ecclesiastical street, the *Rue des Chanoines*, running parallel with the more secular *Grande Rue*, bears in mediæval documents the strange title of *Vetus Roma*, which has been held to point to a still earlier enclosure, that of the primitive Gaulish fort itself. Of the Roman walls, whose construction, like that of most Roman walls in Gaul and Britain, shows them to be not earlier than the third century, large portions still remain; indeed a little time back it might have been said that the river front of the wall, with its noble range of round bastions, was all but absolutely perfect. On the other side, towards the modern town, the wall was less perfect, but even there a great deal could be made out. But the Roman walls did not take in the whole even of the mediæval city. In the thirteenth century an outer range of wall was raised close to the stream, taking in the suburb of *La Tannerie*; an extension to the south and south-east took in the quarter of Saint Ben'et, and another suburb called *L'Epéron*. More remarkably still, at the north-east corner of the Roman inclosure, the growth of the cathedral of Saint Julian to the east, exactly as in the case of Lincoln, overleaped the Roman wall and caused a further enlargement at this corner. It should be noticed that, contrary to the general Gaulish rule, the church of Le Mans stood in a corner of the original city, so as to make somewhat of an ecclesiastical quarter after a fashion English rather than Gaulish. In the Cenomannian state, the Prince, the Bishop, and the citizens all held their distinct places, and it was reasonable that their geographical quarters should be marked also. In fact, in the great days of Cenomannian history the Bishop was a power independent alike of Count and city. He owed temporal allegiance to neither, but held directly of the King at Laon or at Paris. Had the development of things in Gaul followed the same course as the development of things in Germany, Maine might have seen, like so many German lands, the ecclesiastical and the temporal principality and the free city, all side by side, bound together by no tie beyond such degree of dependence as any of them might have kept on the common centre. But when county, bishopric, and city all came under the strong hand of the Norman, all tendencies of this kind were checked. And they perished for ever when Normandy and Maine, instead of external fiefs, became incorporated provinces of the French kingdom.

Within and around the walls of the city there arose in different ages a series of buildings, ecclesiastical, military, and civil, which might claim for Le Mans a place among the cities of Gaul and Europe next after those cities which had been the actual seats of imperial or royal dominion. Above the river rose the double line of walls and towers, Roman and mediæval, and high above them the vast and wondrous pile of Saint Julian's minster. On the side away from the river, the side pointing towards the hostile land of Anjou, built on the Roman wall itself and seemingly out of Roman materials, stood the palace of the Counts, well placed indeed for Count Herbert, *Evigilans Canem*, to sally forth on the nightly raids before which black Angers trembled.[67] And besides the dwellings of the temporal and spiritual chiefs, the ancient streets of Le Mans were set thick with houses, the dwellings of priests and citizens, which showed how well both classes throve, and how each did something for the adornment of the city in every form of art, from Romanesque to *Renaissance*. But a little time back the traveller might have seen at Le Mans more houses of the twelfth century than he would see anywhere north of Venice. And besides the works of her own princes, bishops, and citizens, Le Mans had also once to show the grimmer memorials of her conquerors. But, as not uncommonly happens, the memorials of the earlier time have outlived those of the later. At the northern end of the city William thought it needful to strengthen his greatest continental conquest by two distinct fortresses. Close by Saint Julian's, just outside the eastern line of the Roman wall, and formed, we may believe, out of its materials, rose the Castle, the *Regia turris*. Some way to the north-east, at a greater distance from the river, rose the fortress of *Mons Barbatus* or *Mont Barbet*, this last standing on higher ground than the city and the royal tower. But of the royal tower itself, and of the fortress into which it grew in later times, a few fragments only have escaped the politic destruction of the days of Richelieu. Of Mont Barbet nothing is left but the *motte* or *agger*, dating doubtless from far earlier days, but which, as so often happens, has outlived the buildings which were placed upon and around it. One would have been well pleased to see the whole line of defence, the double wall of the city, the double fortress of the Conqueror, grouping, as they must have done, with the endless towers and spires of the monastic and parochial churches of the city and its suburbs.

For, besides the great cathedral church within its walls, Le Mans was, as it were, girded with great ecclesiastical buildings. Two noble monastic churches, those of La Couture, on the south-eastern side of the city, and of Le Pré, on the other side of the river, still remain; and we have spoken of their architectural character in past years.[68] There were also the Abbeys of Beaulieu, beyond the river, and of St. Vincent opposite to it beyond Mont Barbet, of which the latter survives in the shape of a *Renaissance* rebuilding. And far away in a distant suburb to the east is the hospital founded by the last native prince of Le Mans, the great Henry, to whom his native city might seem as a central point of his vast domain, insular and continental. In him the blood of all the older rulers and enemies of Le Mans was joined together. The stock of the old Counts and of the Norman conquerors, the blood of Helias and of his Angevin representatives, all flowed together in the veins of the King who was born within the walls of Le Mans, and who, if he did not die within its walls, at least died of grief at seeing them in the hands of his enemy.

N.D. du pré Le Mans, N.E.

Notre-Dame-du-Pré, Le Mans, N.E.

But it is painful for one who remembers Le Mans only eight years back to speak of what it is now. It is hard to believe that within that time Le Mans has beheld no slight or unimportant warfare beneath its walls, and that the city of Herbert and Helias bowed but yesterday to the power of a third conquering William. Le Mans has lost something through the foreign occupation, but the traveller needs to have it explained to him what it has lost. When we hear that the Bishop's palace got burned by the German invaders, it almost sounds as if Germans and Normans had got confounded. But the damage wrought by the last conquerors is being speedily made good on another site. It is the damage which is doing to the city by the merciless hands of its own people that never can be made good. One would have thought that the Cenomannian city on its height, the proud line of its Roman bulwarks, the noble works of later days which those bulwarks shelter, might have moved the heart of the most ruthless of destroyers. It might have been a good work to clear away the mean houses which cling to the Roman wall, and to let the mighty rampart stand forth in all its majesty; but among those who have the fate of the ancient city in their hands there is no thought of preservation—destruction is the only object. We know not who are the guilty ones. Perhaps there is some stuck-up Mayor or Prefect who would think himself a great man if he could make Le Mans as ugly and uninteresting as the dreary modern streets of Rouen or of Paris itself. It is at all events certain that M. Haussmann was not long ago seen in Le Mans, and such a presence at such a time is frightfully ominous. At any rate the facts which can be seen by the traveller's own eyes are beyond doubt. The later walls close by the river have been broken down to leave fragments here and there as ornaments in a kind of garden, and, worse still than this, the ancient wall has been broken through, and the ancient city itself cleft in twain. By an amount of labour which reminds one of Trajan cutting through the Quirinal, *la Cité* has been cut into two halves with a yawning gulf between them; the Roman wall is broken through, and the very best of the twelfth-century houses has been ruthlessly swept away. The excuse for this brutal havoc is to make a road or street of some kind direct from the modern town to the river. If the savages could have been persuaded to pay a visit to Devizes, they might there have learned that the claims of past and present may be reconciled. There the simple device of a tunnel carries the railway under the ancient mound without doing the least harm; and a tunnel might in the same way have connected the modern town with the Sarthe without doing the least damage either to Roman walls or Romanesque houses. But there are minds to which mere havoc gives a pleasure for its own sake. A great part of Saint Julian's is more than seven hundred years old, and in the eyes either of Bishop or of Prefect it may be ugly. The vast *menhir* which rests against one of its walls has seen many more than seven centuries, and the most devoted antiquary can hardly call it beautiful. When the Roman walls of Le Mans are not spared, nothing can be safe. All that can be done is for those in whose eyes antiquity is not a crime to run to and fro over the world as fast as may be, and see all that they can while anything is left.

MAINE

1876

WE have already spoken of the capital of the Cenomanni, and some mention of the district naturally follows on that of the capital. In no part of Gaul, in the days at least when Le Mans and Maine stand out most prominently in general history, are the city and the district more closely connected. Maine was not, like Normandy, a large territory, inhabited to a great extent by a distinct people—a territory which, in all but name, was a kingdom rather than a duchy —a territory which, though cumbered by the relations of a nominal vassalage, fairly ranked, according to the standard of those times, among the great powers of Europe. Maine was simply one of the states which were cut off from the great duchy of France, and one over which Anjou, another state cut off in the like sort, always asserted a superiority. Setting aside the great though momentary incident of the war of the *Commune*, the history of Maine during its life as a separate state consists almost wholly of its tossings to and fro between its northern and its southern neighbours, Normandy and Anjou. The land of Maine, in short, is that of the district of a single city, forming a single ecclesiastical diocese. In old times it contained no considerable town but the capital; and even now, when the old county forms two modern departments, with Le Mans for the *chef-lieu* of Sarthe and Laval for the *chef-lieu* of Mayenne, the more modern capital is still far from reaching the size and population of the ancient one. Normandy, with its seven ancient dioceses, its five modern departments, cuts quite another figure on the map. With so many local centres, Rouen never was Normandy in the sense in which Le Mans certainly was Maine; and the strong feeling of municipal life which, as the history of the *commune* shows, must have always gone on at Le Mans, may have tended to make a greater concentration of the being of the whole district in the capital than was found in other districts of the same kind. Add to this, that, though the land of Maine contained but a single diocese, yet that diocese was of much larger and greater extent than any of the seven dioceses of Normandy. This is shown by the fact that, while in the modern ecclesiastical arrangements of France, two of the Norman dioceses have been united with others, the one Cenomannian diocese has been divided into two.

In another point also Maine shows itself very distinctly as a Northern district. This is in its architecture. As Anjou is the architectural borderland between Northern and Southern Gaul, so Maine is again the architectural borderland between Normandy and Anjou. But it shows its character as a borderland, not by possessing an intermediate style, as the Angevin style is distinctly intermediate between the styles of Normandy and of Aquitaine, but rather by using the Norman and Angevin styles side by side. In the nave of St. Julian's itself, an Angevin clerestory and vault is set upon an arcade and triforium which may be called Norman. At *La Couture* the nave has wholly given way to an Angevin rebuilding, while the choir remains Norman, with a touch of earlier days about it. In the third great church of Le Mans, that of *Le Pré*, the Angevin influence does not come in at all. In the department of military architecture, Sir Francis Palgrave says that the familiar Norman square keep was borrowed from Maine; but he brings no evidence in support of this theory, nor have we been able to find any. It seems far more likely that the fashion was originally Norman, and that it then spread into the borderland, and it is certain that some of the most historically famous castles in the land of Maine were the work of Norman invaders.

Maine is, in one point, one of the parts of France in which an Englishman is most inclined to feel himself at home. It shares, though perhaps in not so marked a degree, the same English look which runs through a large part of Normandy and Brittany. It has hedges and green pastures, a sight pleasing to the eye after the dreary look of so many districts of France. The land is also fairly wooded, and the vine, of which we hear so much in our accounts of ancient Cenomannian warfare, is, to say the least, not so prominent a feature as it was then. And we need not say that vines, except either on a hill-side or against a house, do not add to the picturesqueness of a landscape. The land, without being strictly hilly, much less mountainous, is far from flat, and it contains some considerable heights, as the ranges culminating in the peak of Mont Aigu, which forms a prominent object from the theatre at Jublains, and the high ground at and near Le Mans itself, some points of which proved of great importance in the last warfare which Maine has seen. In short, without containing any very striking elevations, there are many sites in Maine well suited for military positions in ancient warfare, sites where the castle has not failed to spring up, and where a town or village has naturally gathered round the fortress. But since the city of the Diablintes was swept from the earth, Maine has, at least till quite modern times, contained no place which can at all set itself up as a rival to the ancient capital. The hill fort which grew into the city of the Cenomanni still remains the undoubted queen of the land of Herbert and Helias.

It is well to enter the Cenomannian county by a point which is Cenomannian no longer, but which not only plays a great part in the local history, but gives a view of a very large part of the land from which it was long ago severed. This is from the hill of Domfront, the fortress and town which the Conqueror wrested from Maine and added to Normandy; but which till the changes of modern times kept a sign of its old allegiance in still forming for ecclesiastical purposes part of the Cenomannian diocese. Domfront, the conquest of William, the cherished possession of Henry, is indeed an outpost of the Norman land, placed like a natural watch-tower, from which we may gaze over well nigh the whole extent of the land which lay between Normandy and the home of the enemy at Angers. Like Nottingham, town and castle stand on two heights, with a slight fall between them, and the town itself is strongly fortified, with a noble range of walls and towers which are largely preserved. The shattered donjon rises on the height where the Varenne runs through a narrow dell between the castle hill and a wild rock on the other side. Castle and town alike equally look out in the direction of danger; from either height it needs no strong effort of imagination to fancy ourselves on the look-out against the hosts of Geoffrey of the Hammer coming from the South. Yet it is at Domfront that the traveller coming from the land of Coutances and Avranches finds himself in one important point brought back to the modern world. After going for many days by such conveyances as he can find, he is there enabled to make his journey into the land of Maine by the help of the railway which leads from Caen to Laval. His first stage will take him to a spot which formed another of William's early conquests, but which was not, like Domfront, permanently cut off from the Cenomannian state.

This spot is Ambrières, a town of the smallest class, hardly rising above a village, but which holds an important place in the wars of William and Geoffrey. There William built a castle, and the shattered piece of wall which overhangs the road running on the right bank of the Varenne may well be a part of his building. The little town climbs up, as it were, to the castle, and contains more than one house bearing signs of ancient date. It is clearly one of those towns which grew up immediately round the fortress. But of the castle itself so little is left that the most striking object now is the church, which stands apart on the other side of the river. A large cruciform building of nearly untouched and rather early Romanesque, it is thoroughly in harmony with the memories of the place. But the church of Ambrières is more than this. It tells us in what direction we are travelling; its aisleless nave, though it would be narrow in Anjou, would be wide in England or Normandy; and there is another feature which looks as if the men of Ambrières had got on almost too fast in their tendencies towards a southern type of architecture. The central tower is indeed low and massive, but so are many others both in Normandy and England; nor would the wooden spire with which it is crowned suggest that in the inside the four plain arches of its lantern support as perfect a cupola as if we were on the other side of the Loire. But both the arches of the lantern and the barrelled vault of the choir keep the round arch. Maine was far off from the land of the Saracen, and the pointed arch would here be a sign that later forms were not far off. From Ambrières either the railway or, if the traveller likes it better, a road leading up and down over a series of low hills, will take him to another scene of William's victories at Mayenne. Here the town slopes down to the river of its own name on both sides, and the castle, instead of crowning either height, rises immediately above the stream. Eight years does much in the way of building up as well as of pulling down; and we may note that since we made an almost casual reference to Mayenne in 1868, [69] the eastern part of the great church, a building remarkable rather for a strange and picturesque outline than for any strict architectural beauty, has had its choir rebuilt on a vast scale after the type of a great minster. No place after the capital has a greater share in the history of the county.[70] It was the lordship of that Geoffrey of Mayenne who played so prominent a part in all the wars of William's day, a part which, both in its good and its bad side, well illustrates the position of the feudal noble. A faithful vassal to his lord, a patriotic defender of his country against an external invader, he could stoop to play the part of a perjured traitor when nobles had been forced to plight oaths against their will to be faithful to a civic *commune*. To the student of the twelfth century Mayenne is full of memories; to the student of earlier times its chief attraction will be that it is the most natural point of the journey to Jublains.

Further down the stream which gives its name alike to the town of Mayenne and the modern department, we come to the one place on Cenomannian ground which, as having become in modern times a seat of both civil and ecclesiastical rule, can alone pretend to any rivalry with the ancient capital. Laval, the *chef-lieu* of the department of Mayenne and the see of the newly founded bishopric, plays no great part in the early history of the district; but though still much smaller than Le Mans, it has fairly grown to the rank of a local capital as distinguished from a mere country town. It is one of the towns which have grown up on a hill and around a fortress,[71] yet it is not a hill city like Le Mans. The old town of Laval, as distinguished from the later suburb on the other side of the river, does not stand on the hill, but climbs up its side. While the *Grande Rue* of Le Mans runs along the ridge, the *Grande Rue* of Laval finds its way up the slope. The castle, as at Mayenne, rises above the river, and still keeps a huge round donjon, patched somewhat, but still keeping several of its coupled Romanesque windows. On the height, hard by a grand town-gate, is the now cathedral church, uncouth enough in the external view, and we may fairly say unworthy of its new rank, but which reveals one of the most instructive pieces of architectural history to be found anywhere. Imbedded in later additions, we still find the choir, transepts, and lantern of a comparatively small Romanesque church, perhaps hardly on a level with Ambrières, but its nave has given way to a vast Angevin nave as wide as the transepts of the original building, and itself furnished with transepts to the west of them. The antiquary will earnestly pray that no one may be led by zeal without discretion to rebuild this church on a scale and style more worthy of its present rank. Let the diocese of Laval, if anybody chooses, be furnished with a new cathedral; but let the present building stand untouched, as one that has undergone changes as instructive as any that can be found.

But the church of the new diocese, though perhaps, by virtue of its singular changes, the most interesting, is hardly the most attractive ecclesiastical building in Laval and its immediate neighbourhood. Not far off in a suburb by the river-side is the church of Our Lady of Avesnières, not improved certainly by its modern spire, but keeping a most stately Romanesque apse with surrounding chapels. Inside it supplies one of the best examples of the transition, the pointed arch having made its way into the great constructive arcades, but not into any of the smaller arches. But the taste of those who designed its capitals must have been singular. Any kind of man, beast, or bird, it has been said, can put himself into such a posture as to make an Ionic volute. When the volutes are made by the heads of eagles, well and good; but it is certainly strange to make them out of the heads of cranes, who are holding down their long necks to peck each one at a human skull which he firmly holds down with one of his feet. And on the other side of Laval will also be found the church of Price, an almost untouched Romanesque building the masonry of which seems to carry it back to days before the growth of either Angevin or Norman taste. And the land of Maine too is full of other spots at which we can barely glance, many of which are famous in the history of the district. On the railway between Laval and Le Mans, Evron has its abbey, with portions both of the earlier Romanesque and of the later Gothic, but where one little transitional chapel on the north side is undoubtedly the most attractive feature of the church. Evron too opens the way to St. Susanne, the one castle which the Conqueror himself could never take, and where the shattered shell of the unconquered donjon, with its foundations raised on a vitrified fort of primitive times, rises on a rocky height, with the stream of the Arne winding in a narrow dell beneath it. Somewhat nearer to the capital, Sillé-le-Guillaume, a spot famous in the war of the *commune*, has a castle and church which should not be passed by, though it is only the under-story of the church which keeps any portions which can belong to the days when Sillé was besieged by the armed citizens of the Cenomannian commonwealth. North of Le Mans, on the upper source of the Sarthe, Beaumont-le-Vicomte keeps the shell of its castle, a castle which long withstood the Conqueror, rising in a lovely position over the river Beaumont, too, has seen warfare in later days, and he who looks down from the castle which withstood the Conqueror may hear the tale of the stout fighting which went on by the banks of the Sarthe, when Maine was invaded by the armies of a later William. The church too with some genuine Romanesque portions, is more curious for a kind of rude *Renaissance* which really reproduces a simple kind of Romanesque. In short, there is hardly a spot in the historic land of Maine which has not its attractions for those who can stoop to scenery which, though always pleasing, is never sublime, to buildings of which perhaps one only in the whole province reaches the first rank, and to a history which, though in itself it is mainly local, has not been without its influence on the destines both of England and of France.

Sainte-Susanne, Keep